The Ghost of the Lantern Lady

The volunteers piled into a wagon filled with hay that was pulled by a large reddish brown horse. The sun was going down, and a breeze rustled the leaves, filling the orchard with dancing shadows.

It got darker and darker as the horse pulled them deeper into the dense orchard. The sweet smell of hay on the cool evening breeze filled Nancy's nose. She leaned back against the edge of the wagon and looked around.

At first all she saw were dark shadows. But then something through the trees caught her eye. It was flickering and bobbing like a huge firefly. She squinted to watch it as the others noticed it and began pointing and murmuring.

Suddenly Bess grasped Nancy's arm tightly. Out from behind a tree floated a figure draped in a pale greenish cloak with billowing sleeves. The face of the figure was concealed by a hood cascading down over the shoulders. Hanging at the end of a long sleeve was a tin lantern. In the light of its flame, the ghostly figure glowed.

Nancy Drew
Mystery Stories

Available from MINSTREL Books

NANCY DREW® 146

THE GHOST OF THE LANTERN LADY

CAROLYN KEENE

A MINSTREL® BOOK

Published by POCKET BOOKS
New York   London   Toronto   Sydney   Singapore

This book is a work of fiction. Names, characters, places and incidents are products of the author's imagination or are used fictitiously. Any resemblance to actual events or locales or persons living or dead is entirely coincidental.

A MINSTREL PAPERBACK *Original*

A Minstrel Book published by
POCKET BOOKS, a division of Simon & Schuster Inc.
1230 Avenue of the Americas, New York, NY 10020

ISBN: 0-671-02663-1

First Minstrel Books printing December 1998

10 9 8 7 6 5 4

NANCY DREW, NANCY DREW MYSTERY STORIES, A MINSTREL BOOK and colophon are registered trademarks of Simon & Schuster Inc.

Front cover illustration by Ernie Norcia

Printed in the U.S.A.

Contents

THE GHOST OF THE LANTERN LADY

1

A Ghostly Surprise

"I always feel as if my car is a time machine when I come here," Nancy Drew said. She stepped out of her Mustang. Its shiny blue color matched her T-shirt and her eyes. "It's as if I've traveled back in time." Her reddish blond hair swung as she shook her head in amazement.

Ahead was Persimmon Woods Pioneer Village, a living-history museum located in the country twenty miles south of River Heights, Nancy's hometown.

"I know," Nancy's friend Bess Marvin said, standing beside the passenger side door. Her blue eyes sparkled with excitement. "It's really going to be fun working here for a week and pretending to be one of the villagers."

1

"Just don't forget," Nancy said, "that our main job is to investigate and gather clues." She remembered her conversation with Anita Valdez, her neighbor from across the street in River Heights. "Anita is sure that all the so-called accidents and thefts here have been caused to cover up the fact that money is being stolen."

"Okay, Nancy, we're ready to help. Aren't we, George? George? Come on."

George Fayne unwound her lanky frame from its curled-up position in the small backseat. "I'm coming," she said. George had short, dark curly hair and brown eyes, and Bess had long blond hair and blue eyes. It would be hard to guess they were cousins.

They headed toward the large igloo-shaped Visitors Center, the only modern building in sight. Inside were a gift shop, theater, restaurant, and museum gallery. Nancy, Bess, George, and the fifteen other volunteers walked the dirt path from the Visitors Center to the one-room log schoolhouse in the village. They sat down on long log benches that ran the width of the room and faced the slateboard wall in front.

"Hi, I'm Cory Worth," said the boy sitting next to Bess on the long bench. He was tall and very cute and looked as if he was about eighteen, Nancy and her friends' age. Thick blond hair hung straight to the shoulders of his T-shirt. His green eyes shone with a friendly gaze. "This is my sister, Amy," he said, nodding to the girl sitting on his other side. "Is this your first time as a volunteer?" he asked Bess.

"Yes," Bess answered. She introduced herself, Nancy, and George. "How about you?"

"Our first time, too," Amy answered. She looked enough like Cory to be his twin, except for her hair. It was long and wavy and a rich dark brown.

The schoolhouse door opened and a woman walked in and went to the slateboard. "My name is Mabel Tansy and I'll be your trainer," she said. "Welcome to your volunteer jobs as Persimmon Woods villagers during the Festival of the Golden Moon. We have two days during which the village will be closed before the festival begins."

She smiled as she paced in front of the slateboard. "I play Mrs. Herman, the doctor's wife," she continued, "and you'll call me by that name during the festival. That's your first lesson and the most important one. While you work here, you will *always* stay in character. Always pretend to be the person you are assigned to be and treat the other villagers as if they are really the people they are playing."

She looked around the group, as if to make sure they understood. Then she smiled. "The rest of the time, please call me Mabel," she said.

3

Nancy thought Mabel looked and sounded just like a woman from the past. She wore a long dress in dark green with a lighter green border and a white apron. Her face was framed with the heart-shaped brim of a bonnet the color of butter.

"We appreciate your help and don't expect you to be experts," Mabel continued. "You don't have to memorize any exact lines. We just want you to act as if you live in 1830. There will always be regular villagers with you. When you're stumped by a tourist's question and you don't know what to say, just let the villagers take over."

Nancy remembered the times she had visited the site on school tours or with family and friends. It was going to be so different this time, living as one of the actual "villagers."

"Many of you have probably visited us before," Mabel said, as if reading Nancy's mind. "You know that we villagers go about our pretend life in spite of the tourists. When it's time to cook our noon meal, we cook it. When the food is cooked, we sit and eat. We treat the tourists as friendly strangers passing through. But we don't let them keep us from our chores and activities."

"When do we find out where we'll be working?" Bess asked. "Do we get to pick the place?"

"We try to assign our regular employees in the areas where they have special skills," Mabel answered. "For these special events, though, I'm afraid you'll have to go where you're needed."

"Now," Mabel continued, "from this moment on, let's take a trip back to 1830s America. There are no cars, no telephones, or television—"

"Yikes! No video games," Cory said with a mock groan. "How did they survive in those days?"

"They made their own fun," Mabel said with a grin. "It didn't come in a box—unless they made the box, too, of course." She motioned them to follow her. "Let's start with a little tour."

Mabel took them through all the buildings in the village. There were twelve log cabins. Most had two rooms. Handmade wood chairs and tables were placed around one room, which was used for living, cooking, and eating. The other room was for sleeping. A few cabins had two rooms with a sleeping loft up above. All were heated with a fireplace and lit by candles. Water came in buckets from the icehouse spring.

"Feel this mattress," Mabel said.

It was lumpy and made a crackling noise when Nancy pushed on it.

"It's stuffed with cornhusks," Mabel pointed out. She lifted up the mattress, which rested on ropes threaded across the bed frame like laces on a sneaker. "After a few nights, these ropes get

5

loose and start to sag," she said, picking up a tool that looked like a wrench made of wood. "You can tighten them with this," she added, twisting the wrench. "Now they don't sag." She smiled, her eyes twinkling. "And that's what the phrase 'Sleep tight' means."

"So that's where that saying came from," George said. "I always wondered what it meant."

Mabel showed the volunteers other buildings besides the residence cabins. They walked through the general store, also made of logs. Its walls were lined with shelves holding fabric and thread, tools and nails, teapots and raw sugar. A large cast-iron stove sat in the middle of the room. The stove was surrounded by rockers and benches, where customers could "sit a spell, store up some heat, and catch up on village gossip," according to Mabel.

The tour continued for the rest of the morning. Mabel walked the volunteers through the barns, which were filled with horses, cows, oxen, and goats. They toured the potter's studio, which had a kiln in the back, and a doctor's wood frame house.

"Now, this is where I'd like to work," Cory said as they entered the blacksmith's workshop.

"The hinges, door pulls, and tools used in the village are made here by our smithy," Mabel said. They all watched as the blacksmith walked over to where he was making a fireplace poker. His fire pit almost looked like a barbecue pit. It was made of bricks and was about waist high. A bellows hung above it. With one strong arm, he pulled on the bellows, forcing air down to fan the flames. His other arm turned the long iron rod that was resting in the flames. The end of the rod glowed yellow-white in the fire.

Then the blacksmith pulled the rod from the flames and placed it on an iron block called an anvil. The end of the rod was so hot that it had become soft. As Nancy and the others watched, he pounded the rod with a huge hammer to flatten and shape it. Each stroke filled the air with an echoing ring and a shower of sparks.

"This is definitely where I want to work," Cory murmured.

Finally Mabel took the group to Windbreak, a large brick house that sat on a small hill next to the village. It had been the original home in the area, built by Brandon Parrish, who had settled there in 1825.

"The windows look a little blurry," Amy said. "The glass has waves in it."

"They are the original windows," Mabel pointed out. "All windows looked like that back then."

Windbreak was quite fancy compared to the rustic cabins they had seen so far. It had woven rugs, wallpaper, and upholstered furniture. There were two rooms plus a large kitchen downstairs. A central staircase led to two large sleeping rooms upstairs. One bedroom was for the parents. There was also a cradle for a baby in that room.

The other bedroom was for the children. Several beds lined one wall, surrounded by old dolls, wagons, and other toys. Clothes were hung on hooks along all four walls. In one corner was a single bed with a little chest and a rocker. "That was for the children's nanny," Mabel explained.

"All right, everyone," Mabel said as they left Windbreak, "let's go outside. We have a small picnic waiting."

Some of the volunteers sat at picnic tables, but Nancy, Bess, George, Cory, and Amy joined others on the soft grass. As they dug into their sandwiches and sodas, they gazed at the village. "Again I feel like I'm drifting back in time," Bess said dreamily.

"Then you should make a great volunteer," Cory said.

"We come here all the time," his sister commented. "I love it here. In fact, I plan to major in history in college, and then I'd like to work full-time in a place like this."

"We've heard there have been some pretty strange things happening around here," Nancy said.

"Yeah, there was a bomb scare phoned in recently," Cory said. "It caused a minor panic."

"And how about the time someone threw all the quilts from the weaver's cabin and the pottery from the kiln into the river," Amy said. "There's been a lot of weird stuff going on."

"That must have been some sight," Cory said. "All those things floating downstream."

"It must have been terrible," Bess said, frowning. "All those beautiful handmade things ruined."

"I think the worst was the musket accident," Cory said. "We were here when it happened, and it was pretty bad."

"Tell us about it," Nancy prompted as she finished her soda.

"Well," Amy answered, "it was during one of the target-shooting competitions they hold here occasionally. One of the muskets misfired and the shooter's hand was burned pretty badly."

"And he was lucky at that," Cory said. "He could have lost an eye. Or worse!"

"But that might have been an accident," George pointed out.

"Not according to the man who was hurt," Amy said. "He swore his musket was tampered with. There was even an investigation, but they just chalked it up to another of the 'unexplained incidents.'"

9

"What about the Lantern Lady?" Cory asked. "Maybe she did it. Oooooeeeeeooooo. The village ghost strikes again."

"The Lantern Lady?" George repeated. "Who's that?"

"Now, never mind about her," Amy said, glancing around quickly. "She's just an old legend. I don't really believe there's such a thing as a village ghost. The people who run this place probably thought her up to bring in the tourists." She smiled, but Nancy could see she was a little nervous.

They finished their lunch, went back to their training until six, and then were ushered back to the barn. "We thought you'd enjoy an evening hayride through the orchard," Mabel said. "Then you'll come back for an authentic pioneer meal by the campfire."

The volunteers piled into a wagon filled with hay that was pulled by a large reddish brown horse. The sun was going down and a breeze rustled the leaves, filling the orchard with dancing shadows.

It got darker and darker as the horse pulled them deeper into the dense orchard. The chattering voices of the volunteers softened to a rustle of whispers. Nancy took a deep breath. The sweet smell of hay on the cool evening breeze filled her nose. She leaned back against the edge of the wagon and looked around.

At first all she saw were dark shadows. But then something through the trees caught her eye. It was flickering and bobbing like a huge firefly. She squinted to watch it as the others noticed it and began pointing and murmuring. As Nancy watched, she felt her nerves dancing just under her skin.

Suddenly Bess grasped Nancy's arm tightly. Out from behind a tree floated a figure draped in a pale greenish cloak with billowing sleeves. The face of the figure was concealed by a hood cascading down over the shoulders. Hanging at the end of a long sleeve was a tin lantern. In the light of its flame, the ghostly figure glowed.

2

Vandals in the Village?

Nancy felt the skin on the back of her neck ripple. No one made a sound as the pale ghost-like figure seemed to float across the wagon path. For a second it was as if all of them—even the horse—were holding their breath.

Then someone in the wagon screamed, and the eerie spell was broken. As suddenly as it had appeared, the ghostly vision was gone.

"Whoa!" the wagonmaster yelled to the horse, pulling hard on the reins. "Easy there!" But the huge horse appeared to have been frightened by the scream. He threw his large head back and shook his thick mane. Rearing up on his back legs, his front hooves jabbed the air.

The orchard was filled with the sounds of

panic as the volunteers were tossed around the wagon. "Hold on," Nancy yelled, grasping the side of the wagon. Stalks of golden hay flew through the air and into the surrounding trees.

The wagon rocked from side to side, then lurched to the right. Bess and Cory spilled out of the wagon like rag dolls and rolled into a shallow ditch full of leaves. Several more volunteers tumbled out after them.

The horse pounded back down onto his two front hooves, tossed his head from side to side, and snorted. "Easy," the driver yelled again, pulling hard on the reins. "Easy there, I said."

The horse's head was hauled back by the tight reins. He shook his mane once again as the driver relaxed his hold slightly. Finally the huge animal calmed down.

"Bess!" Nancy called. "Are you all right?" The horse stepped in place a couple of times but lowered his head and whinnied in response to the driver's continued murmurs.

The wagon finally stopped rocking. Nancy and Amy scrambled off the hay and down into the ditch. The driver left his perch to stroke the horse's head, offering it a few cubes of sugar from his pocket. Then he joined Nancy and the others to check on those in the ditch.

"I think I'm okay," Bess answered, rubbing

13

her shoulder. "Who was that? Or should I say *what* was that? It didn't even look real. It was like a ghost, Nancy—it just floated through the air."

"It was pretty creepy," Nancy agreed. "I don't know what it was." A cloud passed over them, and the orchard became very dark. She strained to see, but there was no sign of the floating figure. The only light came from the flickering lanterns hanging on the sides of the wagon.

Nancy squinted to help her see better and looked around the ditch. "Everyone else okay?" she called. All the others who had been flung from the wagon were standing. Some were brushing leaves and twigs from their jeans and jackets. Others started to climb out of the small ditch.

Cory helped Bess to her feet. "You sure you're not hurt?" he asked, still holding her hand. "How's your shoulder?"

Bess moved her arm gingerly. "Yeah, I'm okay—really." Cory let go of her hand and rubbed her shoulder. Nancy decided Bess was in good hands and began checking on the others. George joined her as they helped people up out of the ditch and back onto the haywagon. There were a few scrapes and scratches, but no one seemed to be seriously hurt.

"I guess we're ready," Nancy told the driver when everyone was settled in the hay.

14

"Please take us back to the village," Bess added, "before that ghost comes back."

"We'll be there shortly," the man answered, clucking gently to the horse.

The wagon ride back was smooth, but everyone chattered nervously about the figure they had seen.

"It sure acted like a ghost," Bess said. "It appeared and disappeared without any warning. Even the horse was spooked."

"A mouse can startle a horse," George pointed out. "That doesn't prove anything. What do you think it was, Nancy?"

"I'm not sure," Nancy answered. "Maybe just another prank," she added. She looked at Bess and George with a slight shake of her head. She knew they'd understand her gesture, warning them not to say any more.

"Well, I agree with you, Bess," Amy said from the other side of the wagon. "It sure looked like a ghost to me."

Everyone was quiet for a moment, then suddenly the silence was broken.

"Oooooeeeeeooooo," Cory moaned in an eerie voice. "Get out of my way, you intruders. I'm the ghost of Persimmon Woods. Oooooeeeeeooooo."

"Stop that," Bess said, dropping a fistful of hay over his head. Amy and a few others joined in and pelted Cory with clumps of hay.

15

"Don't let him get to you," Amy said, grinning at Bess. "He'll do anything for a laugh."

Mabel Tansy was waiting for them when the wagon arrived at the village barn. "Well, now," she said. "Glad to see you made it back safe and sound. It was a beautiful evening for a hayride."

As Nancy watched, the driver left the wagon and pulled Mabel aside. They talked softly. Nancy saw Mabel look at the man in shock, then shake her head slowly. Mabel was frowning as she returned to the group.

"I understand you had a surprise visitor in the orchard," Mabel said. "I'm sorry some of you were frightened. I hope no one was hurt." She looked around the group, still frowning.

"Everyone seems to be okay," Nancy said. "But what did we see exactly? Was it part of the show? An actor, maybe, playing a part?"

"I'm afraid not, Nancy," Mabel answered, shaking her head. "It sounds to me as if—"

"It was the Lantern Lady, that's who," the driver interrupted as he unhitched the horse. "It was her, pure and simple." He mumbled to himself as he worked.

"The Lantern Lady!" Cory said. "Sure sounds like a ghost to me. See, I told you girls. Oooooeeeeeoooooo." Some of the other volunteers moved closer together. A shudder trickled

16

down Nancy's back like the one she felt when she first saw the strange sight in the woods.

"The Lantern Lady makes her appearance occasionally," Mabel continued. "We haven't seen her for a couple of months. The old-timers around here believe that she is the spirit of one of the original settlers. She just checks in now and again to see how times have changed."

"Used to be, that's all it was," the driver grumbled. "Now I'm not so sure. With all the peculiar happenings around here lately, some folks think she's changed her ways and turned to meanness. She's put a hex on this place, and no good will come from that." He turned abruptly and led the horse toward the barn.

Nancy looked around. The group was hushed. Several had startled expressions on their faces. A few seemed frightened by the driver's words.

"Now, now," Mabel said. "Don't pay him any mind. We're all a little skittish lately." She sighed, then smiled. "But we've got a big week coming up, and we need to keep our minds on that. Let's get over to the campfire. The full-time villagers have fixed you a nice supper, and we'll give you your assignments for the festival."

She bustled around the volunteers, herding them over to the fire, which was ringed by handmade log benches. Nancy, Bess, and George

17

joined the others in a line for the tables of authentic Persimmon Woods food. Bowls were heaped with fragrant popcorn, golden-brown roast chicken and potatoes, and apples cooked in brown sugar. Platters were piled with fresh vegetables, homemade bread, and churned butter. Another table held trays of cookies and gingerbread and mugs of frosty cider, cold milk, and hot coffee.

Nancy and her friends joined Cory and Amy on one of the benches. "I didn't realize how hungry I was until I smelled this food," George said.

"Can't let a ghost spoil our appetites, right?" Cory said as he bit into a chicken leg. While they ate, they talked about the Lantern Lady and compared stories about what they'd seen during the hayride. In the background, a few of the full-time villagers played early American folk songs on dulcimers and wooden flutes.

"The weirdest thing was that the Lantern Lady made no sound," Bess said. "I never heard her coming at all. She just appeared."

"We were pretty deep into the orchard at that point," Nancy said. "She could have been hiding behind a tree until the wagon approached. Those old wooden wheels creak and groan a lot. They could have masked any sound she might have made."

"You don't think it *was* a ghost, do you?" George asked Nancy.

"I don't know what—or who—it was," Nancy said. "None of us does." She remembered the eerie feeling she had felt when she saw the figure, and added, "But if it wasn't a ghost, it sure was a good imitation of one."

Mabel climbed up onto one of the benches to ring a cast-iron bell. "Could I have your attention, please?" she called out. "Everyone, settle down for a minute. I would like to give the volunteers their assignments for the festival."

The chatter quieted, and everyone looked toward Mabel. "Thank you," she said with a smile. "Now, let me see." She looked at the clipboard she was holding and adjusted her glasses. Then she read off the list of volunteers and the parts they would be playing for the next week.

Cory was assigned to assist full-time villagers in leading tourists through Windbreak, the large brick house on the hill at the edge of the village. At first he seemed disappointed with his role. But his expression brightened when he learned that Bess would be working with him.

George would portray the daughter of the blacksmith and his wife. She would spend most of the time working with her "mother" in the cabin and part of the time helping her "father" in the smithy's shop.

Nancy would be what Mabel called a floater, which meant that Nancy would "float" from site to site, filling in wherever a villager was needed. Her first assignment would be in the doctor's house, helping Mabel. Nancy would play Mabel's younger sister, visiting from Kentucky.

"You may choose a name to use if you like," Mabel said. "Or you can use your own if it's suitable to the 1830s. I'll be glad to help if you have any questions."

"We've already checked," Amy said. "Cory and Amy are perfect names for those times."

"I think Bess and Nancy will work," Bess said. "But George? For a girl? I don't think so. How about Georgiana?"

"Hmmm, I suppose so," George muttered, taking a long drink of her cider.

After Mabel had read off all the assignments, she led the volunteers back to the Visitors Center. "Tomorrow we will be in costume all day," she said. "Don't be late."

Nancy, Bess, and George talked about the Lantern Lady as Nancy drove them home from the village.

"What if the Lantern Lady really *is* a ghost?" Bess wondered finally. "And she's the one causing all the trouble out there?"

"Well, it sure won't make solving the mystery any easier," Nancy said.

20

All three were quiet for the rest of the drive, lost in their own thoughts.

At eight o'clock Sunday morning, Nancy picked up George and Bess and drove to Persimmon Woods Village for their second day of training. As they approached the employee parking lot, Nancy noticed a small crowd gathered outside the Visitors Center. "Mabel must be late," she said. "Looks like everyone's locked out."

Nancy parked the car, and she and her friends walked over to join the others outside the door. Within a few minutes, Mabel bustled up, sputtering an apology. "I'm so sorry," she said. "My stupid alarm clock failed me again."

Mabel opened the door and the group filed in and headed across the reception area for the stairs to the lower-level dressing rooms and lockers. As Nancy passed the museum gallery, she noticed that its door was open about an inch.

She stopped and peeked through the opening, but it was dark and she saw nothing. "Hello?" she called softly. "Anyone in here?" There was no answer. She gently pushed on the door with her shoulder, but it wouldn't budge.

"What is it, Nancy?" George asked from behind.

"This door was ajar, but no one's in there," Nancy answered. "I'm sure it should be locked.

When I push it, it seems to be stuck," she said. "I'll see if I can find Mabel."

"Here, let me help," Cory volunteered as he joined them. Before Nancy could stop him, he gave the door a hard shove with a shoulder. The door eased open enough for Nancy to slip inside. She felt around for a light switch and flicked it on.

When the light went on, Nancy gasped. The room was in a shambles. Paintings and photographs had been pulled off the walls and thrown around. Display cases were broken open and turned over. Their contents were ripped and smashed. Broken glass, shredded paper, and splintered wood littered the floor. It looked as if a tornado had whirled around the room.

3

The Show Must Go On

Nancy stepped around the fallen display case that had blocked the door shut. She had a sick feeling as she glanced at the room.

"Oh, no," George said softly as she pushed in after Nancy. "Who would have done this?"

"Wow!" Cory added. "What a mess."

Several others including Mabel picked their way through the doorway and into the room. "Not here, too!" she cried.

Nancy turned quickly. "What do you mean?"

"The gift shop," Mabel answered breathlessly. "It's also a mess. We've been robbed. I'll call the police—and Jake."

"Who's Jake?" Bess asked Nancy in a whisper as she joined them.

23

"Jake Parrish," Nancy said softly. "He's the village director. You and Cory take the other volunteers down to the locker room," she suggested. "Make sure everything's okay down there. George and I will stay here until the police arrive. I'm sure they'll want to talk to me since I spotted the open door."

Bess and Cory led the volunteers out of the small gallery. "Let's look around a little," Nancy said to George. "Just make sure you leave everything the way it is. Don't touch anything."

"What are we looking for?" George asked. She sighed as she gazed at the rubble.

"I'm not sure," Nancy answered. "It's going to be hard to discover something unusual or out of place in this mess. I have one question, though."

"What's that?" George asked.

"There's only one door to this room," Nancy pointed out. "If someone ransacked the room and left by that door, how did the display case get knocked over to block it from the inside?"

"Maybe it just fell over," George offered. "It was just an accident that happened afterward."

"Not likely," Nancy said. "Look at the marks on the floor. It was dragged over to the door from that spot against the wall. There has to be another way out."

As they searched for clues, Nancy was startled by a familiar voice at the gallery door. It belonged to Anita Valdez. "I don't believe this! What happened?" she asked.

"Anita!" Nancy said. "What are you doing here on a Sunday?"

"I was going to catch up on a little work," Anita answered quickly. "What an awful mess."

"The gift shop got hit, too," George said. Nancy introduced Anita to George.

George and Anita smiled at each other, then Anita turned to Nancy. "Um, could I speak to you in private, please?"

"Sure," Nancy answered.

"No problem," George said. She carefully picked her way through the rubble to the far corner of the gallery.

"I didn't want to say anything in front of your friend," Anita said in hushed tones. "I'm really here trying to find out what's happening to the money for this place," she added, her eyes darting around nervously. "I've discovered something, and I really don't know what to do about it. I don't want to take any steps until I talk to your father. I really need his counsel."

"He's tied up at a party for an old friend today," Nancy said. "Can it wait till tomorrow? I'm sure he'll fit you in his schedule. Call him this evening—he should be home by seven."

Nancy could hear voices in the hall. People were approaching the gallery door. One of them sounded like Mabel. Anita appeared to hear them, too, and became edgy. "I've got to get out of here," she said, heading for the back of the room. "Don't tell them I was here, Nancy. Please."

Nancy watched while Anita hurried to the back of the room. Suddenly Anita tapped an old iron candle sconce hanging on the wall. With a swoosh, half the wall slid into a pocket in the other half. Anita darted through the large opening, and just as suddenly, the wall swooshed shut. Nancy stumbled across the rubble-littered floor after her. Nancy tapped the sconce as Anita had done, and half the wall slid open again, revealing a large opening into a warehouselike storeroom.

"Cool," George said, as the two peered into the dark back room.

"That door wasn't open before," Mabel Tansy shouted from behind them. "What did you do? How did you open that?" She strode across the gallery to where Nancy and George were standing.

"I touched this candle sconce and it just opened," Nancy said.

"Please leave things alone," Mabel cautioned. "We shouldn't be poking around. The police are on their way, and they should see the room just as we found it. Let's wait in the reception area." Nancy watched her reach around to the store-

26

room wall and push a button. The hidden door slid out and became part of the gallery wall again.

Nancy, George, and Mabel sat on the plush upholstered benches lining the large reception area. Within minutes, two police officers arrived, along with a tall man with curly dark red hair.

"Mabel!" the redheaded man barked. "What happened?" His brown eyes flashed with gold lights.

"We don't know," Mabel answered. "This is Nancy Drew. She's a festival volunteer. Apparently she was the first to discover the gallery door open. Tell Mr. Parrish what you found, Nancy."

Nancy told the village director and the two police officers about the open gallery door and the case pushed against it.

The police officers wrote down her phone number. Then one of them gave her his card and told her to give him a call if she thought of anything else that might help their investigation. The police then went to check the gallery.

As Nancy and George left for the locker room, Nancy overheard Mabel and Jake Parrish talking.

"You've got to cancel the festival," Mabel said. "It's just too much. I can call in some of the regulars, even put the new recruits to work. But we'll never get this cleaned up by Tuesday."

"Absolutely not!" Jake Parrish said in a thundering voice. "I'll hire as many people as it takes

27

to get this mess fixed. The gallery doesn't have to be open by Tuesday, but the gift shop will be ready for customers by ten o'clock that morning. I promise you that!"

Nancy turned back. "I'll be glad to help, Mabel," she said. "I'm sure the rest of the volunteers will pitch in."

"Go tell the others what's happened," Mabel said with a sigh. "We'll train for a couple of hours until the police are through. Then we'll help with the cleanup."

The festival volunteers spent the rest of the morning on the village grounds learning to cook pioneer food over open fires and in beehive ovens, make candles and soap, and play pioneer games. These were all skills they would help demonstrate to the tourists in the week to come.

After a quick lunch, Nancy, Bess, and Cory helped clean up the museum gallery. George and Amy assisted with a similar mess in the gift shop.

Nancy asked her friends to watch for clues in case the police missed any. She told Bess and Cory about the hidden sliding door in the back wall.

"I should have realized there was another opening," Nancy said. "There was no way the entry door could have been the only way in. All museums have large doorways so large objects can be moved for exhibitions."

"You have to figure the vandals knew about that door if they escaped that way," Cory said. "They must have known their way around here."

"Or they accidentally hit the candle sconce while they were trashing the place," Nancy pointed out.

"It's so sad to see all this damage," Bess said. "Look at this. They must have had a display of textile arts in here this month. All these beautiful pieces." She held up fragments of cloth. Some were embroidered with birds and flowers. Some had beautiful lace borders. A few were scraps of woven blankets. All of them looked very old.

"This looks like a family tree," Bess said. She pieced together a piece of yellowed material from the torn strips she found on the floor. It was like working a jigsaw puzzle. Cory and Nancy helped, but the cloth was so old, none of them could read the embroidered names on the tree branches.

"I remember that piece," one of the full-time villagers said. "It was framed and hung right here." She pointed to a hook on the wall. "It was so difficult to read that one of the museum restorers made a drawing of it recently so we could read the names. The drawing hung next to the sampler, but I don't see it now," she added, looking around. "Probably destroyed it, too."

While they worked, Nancy and her friends

watched for the paper drawing of the family tree, but never found it.

A relief cleanup crew showed up about three o'clock. The festival volunteers took a break for cookies and soda, then went downstairs to the dressing rooms and lockers on the lower level.

Along the walls of the dressing rooms were costumes hanging on poles. On the floor were boxes of shoes and boots, hats and bonnets, belts and ties for the men and boys, large white collars for the women and girls, and suede pouches of several sizes. Each volunteer was assigned a locker and told to pick a costume.

"Ordinarily, you would have worn your costume all day," Mabel told them. "These outfits take a little getting used to when you're moving around."

Nancy, Bess, George, and Amy picked similar dresses. They had long full skirts worn over a full white petticoat. Bess's silk dress had an extra ruffle about twelve inches up from the hem and was a beautiful flower print on a pale yellow background. Nancy and Amy picked solid colors—Nancy blue, and Amy red. George's dress was green with a tiny navy blue stripe.

As they dressed, Nancy pulled George aside. "Did you find anything in the gift shop when you were cleaning up?" Nancy asked.

"Nope," George said. "Just a big mess. No one

seemed to think anything was stolen. There wasn't any money in the cash register to begin with. So it must have just been vandalism. It's really pathetic."

Nancy and George rejoined the others and finished dressing. All the dresses had full sleeves and large white collars. Bess and Nancy both wore fabric belts at their waists.

All four girls picked out bonnets. Nancy and Amy chose straw ones with broad brims that tied under their chins with wide ribbons. George wore a simple plain white caplike bonnet with a self tie. Bess picked out a hat that surrounded her face in a heart-shaped frame and tied with a big blue bow.

"Outstanding!" Cory said, looking them over.

"You don't look so bad yourself, brother dear," Amy said as she walked around him.

Cory wore gray pants with a striped vest and a short jacket with tails and a velvet collar. His white shirt had a small collar that stood up around his chin. Serving as a tie was a wide black band that tied in a small bow in the front. A tall gray hat perched on his blond head.

"Thank you, my dear," he said with a bow. "Shall we take a stroll, miss?" He took Bess's hand and tucked it under his arm. The two walked gracefully around the room as the others watched.

31

"There's something about these clothes," Bess said as they strolled back. "They make me feel different. As though I really lived back then."

"There's something about them all right," George said. "They're too tight and too long and too weird."

"Don't complain." Nancy grinned. "You look wonderful."

With their costumes on, the volunteers worked at their assigned sites for the rest of the afternoon, guided by Mabel and other full-time villagers. Finally the day's training was over and all the volunteers were dismissed.

Nancy and her friends were surprised at how tired they felt on the drive home. Finding the vandalism and cleaning it up had made the day seem longer.

After taking Bess and George home, Nancy pulled into her driveway just before her father did.

Carson Drew put an arm around her shoulders as they walked into the house. "Ooh, careful, Dad," Nancy said. "My shoulders are pretty achy. I thought I knew how hard the early Americans worked, but I really didn't have a clue."

"You've been finding out, I take it," her father said.

"You said it," she answered. "They work harder

fixing one dinner than most people these days do fixing a whole week of meals."

"And was it worth it?" Carson asked, putting his briefcase down.

"The food's good," Nancy said, laughing. "But give me pizza, tacos, and a microwave any day."

As Nancy told her father about the destruction in the gallery and gift shop, she felt the day's tension leave her. She was always reassured when she talked to her dad and bounced ideas off him.

"You're right," Carson said, when she had finished. "It is getting hard to keep up with the village's problems. Be very careful while you're working there. Stay alert. I don't want anything to happen to—"

"Carson! Nancy!" Anita Valdez ran into the room. "Hi," she said, giving them an embarrassed smile. "Hannah let me in. I'm sorry to burst in on you like this, but I had to talk to you. You're not going to believe what's happened. I've been fired!"

4

A Sound in the Shadows

"Fired!" Nancy said. "Why?"

"Oh, I knew this was going to happen," Anita said. "I'm sorry to storm in like this, but I didn't know where to turn."

"Have a seat, Anita," Carson said. "Tell us what happened."

Anita spilled out her story quickly. Nancy thought it looked as if the young woman was choking back tears.

"Remember I told you that I suspected something funny was going on at Persimmon Woods?" Anita told the Drews. "Not out in the village, although there's plenty of weird stuff there. But I'm talking about in administration—especially in accounting."

"You told me you had something you wanted to ask my father about," Nancy prompted.

"That's right. Now I think it's all related—the suspicious accounting and the so-called accidents in the village. Someone is sabotaging the place—I'm sure of it."

"But who?" Nancy asked. "Who would do it? And why?"

"Jake Parrish, that's who!" Anita said. "Jake's a descendant of Brandon Parrish, the founder of the original settlement back in 1825. Jake's grandfather, Brandon the third, devised the idea of restoring the buildings and creating Persimmon Woods Pioneer Village as a living-history museum. He wanted to leave a gift to the state and decided to form a nonprofit foundation to restore and run the family property as an educational endowment."

"Jake Parrish gets a good salary to be director," Carson said. "I run into him all the time at fund-raisers and benefits. He's definitely a prime player in the cultural and art community in the area. If he's stealing money from his own family foundation, he's in a lot of trouble."

"You're right—he makes plenty," Anita said, nodding. "But maybe it's not enough. I'm sure he's embezzling from the foundation. I haven't had a chance to check all the figures, but it looks

35

as though it might be close to a hundred thousand dollars."

"But why?" Nancy asked again.

Anita's dark eyes flashed with anger. "I don't know why, but it has to be him. He's the only one with access to the books and the money besides me."

"At least it's not the Lantern Lady," Nancy said.

"The ghost of Persimmon Woods?" Anita said. "Hardly. I've never seen her, but I've talked to people who have. Who knows what that is. I think the villagers keep the legend going because the tourists love it—most of them anyway."

"I'm one of the ones who've seen her," Nancy said. She told Anita about the ghostly appearance during the hayride.

"Well, if she's stealing money from the village, she's sure not a ghost," Anita said.

"Do you have any proof about Jake Parrish embezzling?" Carson asked gently. "Anything that will back your suspicions?"

"No," Anita said, her voice trembling. "That's why I've been hanging out there after hours. I'm trying to pull together the proof I need. I make all the entries in the accounting records, and I make a copy for myself as a backup. I noticed that some of the figures were different from what I remembered. I checked them against the back-up. Some of the official records have definitely been altered. Someone's changed the numbers that I entered."

Anita took a moment to catch her breath, then continued. "But Jake must have figured out what I was doing," she continued. "He fired me today with no notice. He even had a security guard escort me to the door and off the premises. I didn't get to clear out my office, and I wasn't allowed to take anything with me. Jake said he'd have my personal things sent to me."

Anita stayed awhile longer. When she finally left, she was still very upset.

"If Anita's right, I feel really sorry for her, Dad," Nancy said as they finished the light supper their housekeeper, Hannah Gruen, had prepared.

"I do, too," Carson replied. "But she'd better be able to back up her suspicions with hard evidence. Embezzling is a serious crime, especially from a nonprofit foundation—one that's set up to provide learning and fun for the public." Carson looked at Nancy intently. "You go back to the village tomorrow, don't you?"

"Yes," Nancy answered. "The village is closed—it's always closed on Mondays. But we go in for two hours in the morning. All the full-time villagers will be there. We'll do run-throughs of typical conversations and demonstrations before the tourists start flooding the place on Tuesday."

"Well, be careful," her father warned. "Keep your eyes open."

"I will, Dad," Nancy said. She reached up and kissed his cheek. "Thanks."

Nancy went to her bedroom and called George. She told her about Anita's visit. "What if Anita is right?" George said. "Could Jake Parrish really be behind the problems at the village— even the so-called accidents and other scary events?"

"I don't know," Nancy replied. "Anita seems very positive. If only she'd been able to gather the proof before she was fired."

They talked awhile longer before hanging up. George said she'd call Bess and fill her in on Anita's visit. In bed later that night, Nancy tossed and turned. Even though her muscles were tired, her mind just wouldn't settle down.

Nancy sat up. "Maybe I can get the evidence for Anita," she said aloud. "Somehow I've got to get into those accounting records." She lay back down and snuggled into her pillow.

The next morning Nancy, Bess, and George reported to the locker room at ten o'clock. All

38

the villagers dressed quickly and reported to their assigned stations.

Nancy walked down the path to the one-story, wood-frame doctor's house. As she started to open the white wooden gate, she thought she saw a familiar figure lurking by a toolshed behind the house. The sun was in her eyes so she couldn't be sure, but it looked like Anita!

Now, what would she be doing here? Nancy wondered to herself. She's been ordered to stay off the premises. Nancy hurried around the house to the toolshed, but no one was there.

Mabel was in the parlor when Nancy entered the doctor's house. "Good," Mabel said. "Let's get to work." She walked Nancy through the doctor's office with all its scary-looking tools and instruments. Then they went through the parlor and dining room. Both rooms were pretty, with brightly painted floors, wallpaper in lively patterns, and fancy furniture. A small piano sat against one wall in the parlor. The dining room had a large round table with matching chairs.

"I've asked the blacksmith's family to come by in a while," Mabel said. "We'll pretend they're tourists and rehearse our talks about pioneer cooking. Why don't I explain the spit and you describe the beehive oven."

"Fine," Nancy said, hoping she would remember everything she had learned.

39

The blacksmith and his wife and George, playing their daughter, Georgiana, came in about a half hour later.

"Good day," Mabel said, slipping into her character. "Welcome. I'm Mabel, Doctor Herman's wife. This is my sister, Nancy, visiting from Kentucky," she added, nodding to Nancy.

"Where's the doctor today?" the blacksmith asked.

"He's out to one of the villagers on a house call," Mabel answered. "Hope it's not as long as yesterday's. That one was a two-chicken visit."

"What does that mean?" George asked.

"Why, land sakes," Mabel said. "That means the doctor was paid with *two* chickens, instead of just one like an ordinary house call."

Nancy caught George's eye and they both grinned.

"And here's what we're cooking them on," Mabel added, pointing to an odd device. A wheel about the size of a plate hung on the front of the hearth. Mabel grasped the handle on the wheel and gave it several turns. She was actually winding up a long chain that was wound around the wheel. As she turned, a heavy weight that was on the end of the chain was pulled up to the wheel. It reminded Nancy of Hannah's setting her old-fashioned cuckoo clock each night by pulling up the chain weight.

Mabel stopped winding the wheel, saying, "As you can see, the wheel is starting to unwind now, very slowly. It will take two hours for the wheel to unwind and the weight to reach the floor. But it's a real time-saver for the cook."

She pointed to a long iron rod called a spit stretched across the fire with two large chickens threaded on it. The spit was connected to another iron rod, which was connected to the slowly turning wheel. As the wheel turned, it turned the spit. "Our chickens will be perfectly roasted and golden on all sides," Mabel said, "and we won't have to turn them."

As if on cue, the blacksmith's wife asked another question that Nancy might expect from a tourist. "Where do you do your baking?"

Mabel turned to Nancy. Nancy took a deep breath and said, "We use this beehive oven." She opened a door about two feet wide by two feet tall located halfway up the wall. "You probably noticed the oven as you walked up—the large round brick dome on the outside of the house. That serves as a hood, holding in the heat and releasing it slowly through air vents. We cook all our bread and cakes in it—many at a time."

Mabel and Nancy escorted the visitors through the rest of the house, chatting as they played their parts. Other villagers stopped in, giving Nancy plenty of rehearsal.

The morning flew by. By the time Nancy and her friends had changed into their jeans, T-shirts, and jackets, everyone else had left the locker room.

"I want to see if I can check out Anita's old office," Nancy told Bess and George. They lingered a few more minutes, making sure no one came back to the locker room.

"Cory and Amy want us to join them at Rocko's for lunch," Bess said. "I told them we had some errands to run and might not make it."

"We might be able to, if I can get what I need from Anita's office. I'm not going to push my luck and stay any longer than I have to. Anita said the offices are on the second floor, above the reception area and gallery," Nancy told Bess and George. "Hers is the third door from the stairway."

"How are you going to get in?" George asked. "They're probably locked."

"I don't know yet," Nancy answered. "I'll just see what the layout is."

"How about the guard?" Bess asked.

"He's usually in the reception area," Nancy said. "He's really nice. You two go up to the first floor and talk to him. Keep him busy. Tell him you're waiting for a friend. I'll go on up to the offices on the second floor."

"Okay, but don't stay too long," Bess said.

"Everyone's kind of paranoid since the break-ins yesterday. I don't want to get into trouble."

Nancy stayed behind the first-floor stairway door until she heard her friends talking to the guard. Then she hurried up to the second floor. The hall was dark except for the green Exit sign leading to the stairs. She counted three doors to reach the one that had been Anita's.

She wasn't surprised to find the office door locked, but she was disappointed to see that the lock-pick she carried wouldn't work on that lock. Then she noticed that it was an old-fashioned door with a large transom window along the top. Hannah had pointed one out to her once. The window had hinges on its top edge so it could be opened. Hannah had told her that before air-conditioning, the window in the door provided a way to let air flow through the room.

Nancy jumped up to try to reach the window, but it was too high. She raced down the hall to the rest room, where she found a chair. Standing on the chair, she could easily reach the transom window. With a gentle push, the window opened into the office.

Carefully Nancy hoisted herself up and pushed herself feet first through the window. She hung from the bottom edge of the opening on the other side of the door. Then holding her breath, she dropped to the floor inside the office.

She decided to risk turning on the low desk lamp. The light's beam lit up a desk sign reading Treasurer.

Nancy went behind the desk. She knew she had to work fast in case someone came down the hall and saw the chair and open transom. Her pulse pounded in her neck as she checked the desk drawers. They were locked. She turned on the computer. Within seconds she was searching through the files for the accounting records.

A slight rustle in the shadows of the corner made her stop typing. Her breath caught in her throat. She sat very still, her fingers poised above the keyboard. Goosebumps prickled her arms as she realized she was not alone in the dark office. Before she could wheel around, someone grabbed her from behind.

5

An Eerie Warning

Nancy gagged as she felt a hand cover her mouth. She tried to twist free, but the person's other arm held her in a tight grip and pulled her off the chair. Nancy tried to plant her feet to keep her balance. With a sinking feeling, she felt herself being pulled backward through a door and into another room. Although the room was unlit, sunlight filtered through a small dusty window. Nancy saw what looked like piles of boxes and crates. A musty odor filled her nose. It smelled as if they were in an old attic.

Nancy twisted again in an effort to break free, but it was too late. With a sudden, sharp push, she was flung forward into a small dark closet. The closet door was slammed shut and locked with a key. It was very quiet for a moment. Nancy held her breath.

At last she heard footsteps leading away from the closet. Nancy let her breath escape with a whoosh of relief.

Even though she no longer heard anything, she waited a few more minutes. Finally she thought it was safe. She took her lock-pick out of her jeans pocket and used it to open the door of the closet.

Nancy looked around. As her eyes got used to the dim light from the window, she realized she was actually standing in a loft above a room. She walked to the loft railing and looked over at the storeroom that was behind the museum gallery. It was the same room she and George had discovered by opening the sliding panel door.

Quickly Nancy ran alongside the railing until she found a winding staircase that led down into the warehouse. When she got to the main floor of the storeroom, she walked around the edge, sliding her hand along the wall. Finally, she found the button that Mabel had pushed earlier to activate the sliding door.

The wall slid into its pocket, and Nancy stepped into the back of the museum gallery. She tapped the candle sconce to slide the wall closed again. Then she hurried across the gallery to the door leading to the reception area. She unlocked it, reset the lock, and peeked out.

She heard George and Bess talking to the guard. But she could tell they were in the hall around the corner, out of sight. Nancy stepped out of the gallery and quietly pulled the door closed.

She took a deep breath and brushed the dust from her clothes. Then she walked around the corner to where her friends were. They seemed surprised to see her coming from that direction rather than from the stairway. She smiled quickly, saying, "Well, I'm ready. Let's go."

The guard walked Nancy and her friends to the Visitors Center main door. Within minutes, the three were back in Nancy's Mustang and headed for lunch at Rocko's Tacos.

"Oh wow!" Bess said, when Nancy told them what had happened. "Who do you suppose it was?"

"I don't know," Nancy said as she pulled into Rocko's parking lot. "But it sure wasn't a ghost. I do have some clues. Did you two see anyone in the hall while I was gone?"

"No one but the guard," George answered.

"Okay," Nancy said, nodding toward the restaurant. "Amy and Cory are still here. It looks as if they waited for us. I don't want them to know about this."

"Um, Nancy, they already know a little," Bess said.

"What do you mean?" Nancy asked.

"Well, I was going to tell you about it, but I hadn't gotten around to it yet. Cory and I were talking about the Lantern Lady and all the stuff that's been happening out here. I sort of let it slip that you're a detective and we're working on the case. He and Amy think it's really cool. They promised not to tell anyone else, and they even offered to help. That's probably why they're still here, waiting for us."

"Bess," George groaned. "What if they let it slip to someone else? Maybe that's why Nancy got caught in Anita's office."

"It's okay, Bess," Nancy said. "If they really want to help, they won't tell anyone. You didn't tell them about Anita and the embezzling suspicions, did you?"

"Oh, no," Bess said. "We just talked about the incidents in the village and whether the Lantern Lady is causing them or not."

"Okay, let's leave it at that," Nancy said. "Nothing about Anita or Jake Parrish or the money. We can't betray Anita's confidence." She started to open the car door.

"Wait," George said. "Before we go in. You said you had some clues about the person who grabbed you."

"Oh, right. Whoever it was, he or she was left-handed," Nancy said.

48

"How could you tell?" Bess asked.

"Remember, I was grabbed from behind," Nancy said. "The person covered my mouth with the left hand first. So that must be the lead hand. I could tell it was the left hand because I felt the thumb along the left side of my nose."

Amy and Cory waved to them, and Nancy, Bess, and George went into Rocko's.

"Good day, my fine ladies," Cory said. "You're here at last, even though it's nigh onto half-past three." He stood and bowed to them.

"You are taking your part entirely too seriously," Amy said. "Sit. Eat."

Cory pulled Bess's chair out with a flourish, then sat down in the chair next to hers. "So, Nancy," he said, "Bess tells me you're a detective trying to solve the mystery of the problems at Persimmon Woods. How can we help?"

"What about the vandalism of the gallery and gift shop?" Amy chimed in. "Do you have any ideas about that?"

"No, not really," Nancy said. "I don't have anything definite yet. But I appreciate your offer to help. Just keep your eyes and ears open. Let me know if you see anything weird or anyone suspicious hanging around. And please don't tell anyone else about what we're doing."

"No way would we tell," Cory said. "We really want to help."

"He means it," Amy said. "We love the village. Our mom used to take us when we were little, and it seems as if we've been going there all our lives. We would hate to see it destroyed or shut down." She took a sip of her soda and smoothed her long dark hair away from her face. Nancy believed her.

"You know," Amy said, her head tilted, "I did see someone creeping around the back of the Visitors Center just before we left today. He didn't look right."

Nancy put down her taco and leaned over the table. "How do you mean?" she asked. "What made you suspicious?"

"Oh, he was sort of big, and he had dark hair," Amy said. "I don't know. I hadn't seen him around the village before. There was just something about the way he was creeping around— like he didn't want anyone to see him."

"Was he wearing a ring?" Nancy asked.

"I wasn't close enough to see," Amy answered.

"Why, Nancy?" Cory asked, taking a big bite of burrito.

"I was grabbed from behind today around that area," Nancy said, avoiding any details about Anita's office. Quickly Nancy repeated her guess that the person was left-handed and explained why. "There was a ring on the left index finger," Nancy added. "It had a scroll pattern. I could see

50

it out of the bottom of my eye when he clamped his hand over my mouth."

"You said *he* just then," George noted. "So you think it might have been the man Amy saw?"

"I did say *he*, didn't I," Nancy said, as the waitress refilled her soda. "I can't really be sure, though. Whoever it was was pretty strong."

"Well, we hate to leave you ladies, but we have to get home," Cory said. "My mom needs the van. Let us know if you think of something more we can do. We want to help—really."

"Thanks," Nancy said. "Amy, if you remember anything else about that guy, let me know." She handed Amy her phone number.

The Worths left and Nancy, Bess, and George finished their lunch. "If the guy who grabbed you was the one Amy saw, what do you suppose he was after?" George asked Nancy.

"Maybe he was looking for the same information I was and wanted me out of the way," Nancy said. "If that was it, it worked. I didn't get a chance to find out much."

"Well, then, it couldn't have been Jake Parrish," George pointed out. "He has access to those records any time he wants."

"Maybe someone does know you're working under cover to look into the problems at Persimmon Woods," Bess said. "Maybe that someone was trying to warn you to stop your investigation.

I'm sure Cory and Amy wouldn't tell anyone, though."

"I agree, Bess," Nancy said. "I think they really want to help. You know, I thought I saw Anita on the grounds this morning. But when I followed her, no one was there."

"I thought she was ordered to stay away," Bess said.

"She was," Nancy said. "That's why I tried to chase her down."

"But you don't think she's the one who grabbed you in the office, do you?" asked George.

"No," Nancy said. "But did I really see her this morning? If so, what was she doing here?"

"My head is spinning," Bess said, pushing away the rest of her taco salad. "Too many questions, not enough answers."

"And I have the remedy for that," Nancy said, pulling out money for their meal. "Let's go to my dad's office."

They were in downtown River Heights in less than a half hour. "What are we going to find here?" George asked as Nancy parked the car behind Carson Drew's law office.

"My dad has the most complete law library in the area," Nancy pointed out. "Any piece of legal history we want is here, either in books or on computer disks. I want to check out the legal background of Persimmon Woods Pioneer Village. Let's find out how it was set up, how it's financed, and who all the executives are—everything."

"Easy," Bess said. "Point me to the computer. I'll find just the database you need."

Carson's secretary led them to a small private room with a desk, table, and computer. Within minutes Bess had called up the electronic files they needed.

"Mmmm, that's interesting," Nancy said as she read the file. "A man by the name of Leo Meier was the original director of the village. Jake Parrish ran the nonprofit foundation that managed it. I'm sure that Jake is director of both now."

They finished looking through the legal records but found nothing else that helped.

"Bess, let's log onto the on-line newspaper files," Nancy suggested.

Bess searched through the Internet for the library files of the *River Heights Times.* Using the keyword Persimmonwoods, she called up a file that included all articles that had been published about the village in the local newspaper.

They found two that were especially interesting. One explained what happened to Leo Meier, the original director of the village. He had been let go after his initial three years. That was when

Jake Parrish took over as sole director of the village and the foundation.

Meier had sued the village and Parrish, saying that they had verbally promised him that he would be director for seven years even though he didn't have a written contract. Meier eventually did drop the suit.

Another article said that Parrish had recently been approached by a developer who was interested in buying the village. The developer wanted to close it down to build a small private airport. "It will never happen!" Parrish stated firmly.

Nancy printed out some of the information. Then she, Bess, and George finished the afternoon with some shopping. On the way home, they talked about the next day and the festival opening.

"I can't wait," Bess said. "I love my dress, and Windbreak is such fun to tell tourists about. It's a wonderful old house."

"I'll bet some of your excitement has to do with your volunteer partner, Cory Worth," George teased. "He's pretty cute."

Bess smiled, but didn't answer.

At home that evening Nancy called Anita Valdez and asked her about Leo Meier. "We were all surprised when he left," Anita said. "He was an okay guy, and he and Jake had been friends and business associates for years. I think they were even college roommates."

"So why was he let go?" Nancy asked.

"I don't know," Anita said. "I never talked to Jake about it, but the story is that they had different ideas about how to expand and promote Persimmon Woods. Jake wanted to go slow to stay very authentic—the way the village is now. Leo Meier wanted to make it flashier by adding attractions like waterslides and theme rides."

"That *is* different," Nancy agreed. "Do you know what happened to Meier?"

"The last I heard he was working in a museum in Europe somewhere," Anita said. "I really haven't heard his name mentioned for over a year."

"Well, thanks for your help," Nancy said. "Oh, by the way, I saw you at the village this morning. Behind the doctor's house."

"What do you mean?" Anita said. "I wasn't there. I wasn't."

"It's okay, Anita," Nancy said. "I won't tell anyone."

"Nancy, I wasn't there. Period. Now, if you'll excuse me, there's a TV show I want to see." Anita hung up abruptly.

"Well, that was interesting," Nancy muttered. Before leaving the room, she checked her answering machine for messages.

There was only one. First there was just the scratchy sound of static, then a low, muffled voice that sounded far away. "Stay away from Persimmon Woods," the voice said. "There is nothing for you there but danger."

6

A Ghostly Welcome

Nancy felt cold. The voice was low and eerie. It sounded as if it came from another world. She listened to the threatening phone message once more to see if she recognized the voice, but it was impossible. She took out the tape and dropped it in a drawer in case she needed it for evidence later.

She jumped into bed and pulled the covers up high around her neck. She could still hear the creepy warning in her head. If a ghost could talk, Nancy thought, it would sound pretty much like that voice.

Then she thought of the strong person who had wrestled her into the storage-room closet. "That was no ghost," she mumbled. "Whoever you are, you're not scaring me away from this investigation."

Tuesday morning the gates opened to the Persimmon Woods Pioneer Village Festival of the Golden Moon. From the surrounding hillsides, booming cannons and musket fire heralded the entrance of the tourists.

Nancy was very busy at the doctor's house, playing the part of Mabel's younger sister visiting from Kentucky. As the tourists filed through the house, Nancy and Mabel acted as if they really lived there. They did the daily chores and activities of people living during that time, and they answered questions as they had practiced during their run-throughs and rehearsals.

Most of the morning was spent preparing food. Mabel explained to the tourists that they were expecting the blacksmith and his family for dinner about noon so it would be a "company" meal.

Nancy helped Mabel pick vegetables from the garden behind the house. Then she went to the springhouse to get cheese and milk. The springhouse was a small building over a natural spring-fed stream. The water was icy cold, even in summer. The pioneers kept crocks of cheese and tins of milk in the water to keep them cool.

In the winter the springhouse stream froze, and they could store even more foods for longer periods. But even on the hottest day of summer, it was a great place to chill a watermelon.

At noon other villagers stopped in to join Mabel and Nancy for the noon meal. As the tourists came and went, Mabel, Nancy, and their company ate a meal of roast beef, vegetables, and biscuits and blackberry jam. For dessert they had cheese, more biscuits, and wild plums and crab-apples cooked in maple syrup.

They took time between bites to talk to the tourists and tell them about their lives.

After lunch Nancy cleaned up the kitchen. When she finished, she wandered through the dining room into the front parlor. Mabel was by the front door, hugging a large, dark-haired man. Nancy watched as Mabel and the man talked quietly for a few minutes. Then the man left.

"Well, what a surprise to see *him*," Mabel said to Nancy as she watched the man from the parlor window.

"Who was it?" Nancy asked.

"That was Leo Meier," Mabel said. "He used to run things here. Been gone about a year. I'd heard he was working in Europe. I'm real surprised to see him here."

"Is he moving back to America?" Nancy asked.

"He didn't say," Mabel said. She frowned as if she were deep in thought.

Nancy remembered reading about the trouble between the man Mabel had hugged and Jake Parrish. What *was* Leo Meier doing back in town, Nancy wondered. She thought of the man Amy had seen acting suspicious the day before. Could it have been Leo Meier? He fit the description, but so did lots of other men.

In the late afternoon the villagers and the tourists gathered at the river for the reenactment of the twilight arrival of the traders. During the early 1800s, it was traditional for three groups to meet to trade their wares during the Festival of the Golden Moon.

The first group was comprised of residents of Persimmon Woods Village who had worked for months on their offerings. The women wove linen and wool into fabric, sewed quilts, and prepared canned and potted foods. The men made wood furniture and pottery and smoked hams and sausages. Even the children and young people contributed by gathering mushrooms, herbs, and feathers in the woods.

The second group of traders were members of the Miami and Pottawatami tribes of Native

Americans, who came down the river in canoes. They brought handmade jewelry with bright-colored beads and stones, carved wooden dolls and animals, and woven blankets and rugs.

The third group of traders were French Canadians called voyageurs. They also came to the village in canoes, bringing furs, leather pelts, spices, and lace.

Nancy, Bess, and George hurried to the bank of the Muskoka River a few minutes before the traders were scheduled to appear. Cory and Amy joined them soon after. "Nancy, I think I may have seen that man again," Amy said. "The one I saw at the Visitors Center yesterday."

"Nice going, Sis," Cory said. "You'll be a detective yet."

"Where did you see him?" George asked.

"Well, I was delivering some thread from the general store to the potter's wife after lunch," Amy said. "I saw him walking up the path. He might have come from the doctor's house, but I'm not sure. I hurried to get closer. And guess what!"

"He wears a ring on the index finger of his left hand," Nancy said.

"That's right!" Amy said. "How did you know?"

"Just a lucky guess," Nancy said.

"An experienced guess," Bess said proudly. "Nancy's the best."

Nancy didn't mention that it might have been Leo Meier, the man Mabel had greeted. She didn't want to bring up the money angle of this mystery in front of Cory and Amy.

The sun was just beginning to set. "What a sight," Nancy said, looking around. "Just look at all the people."

Tourists and villagers lined the riverbank. In the meadow next to the village, some villagers had constructed simple lean-tos—small open sheds. All the things they had to sell were laid out on tables in the sheds.

When the French and Native American traders arrived, they would be spending the evening setting up their overnight camps in the meadow next to the sheds. They would live there the rest of the week, just as the original traders had. The goods they brought would be for sale—to the tourists as well as the villagers.

"What's that?" Bess asked. "Do you hear music?"

"Yeah," Cory said with a nod. "Someone's singing."

"In French," George added. She turned toward the bend of the river. "Here they come!"

Musket fire heralded the arrival of the traders.

From around the river bend, a parade of sixty canoes drifted into view. Some carried Native American families dressed in beautiful fringed leather clothes and beaded jewlery. Flickering lanterns hung off the front of the canoes like headlights.

Other canoes carried the voyageurs. The men wore floppy black wool caps pulled down on one side and tight black trousers and boots. Bright-colored tunics were belted at their waists with striped sashes. The women wore pretty flowered dresses. The voyageurs sang French folk songs as the procession approached.

"Wow!" Bess said breathlessly. "It's beautiful. I love it!"

Bess's words were joined by the oohs and ahhs of the tourists along the riverbank. The lights on the canoes were reflected in the water, doubling the sparkle effect.

As Nancy watched the canoe procession, all the flickering lanterns and reflections of them seemed to play a trick on her eyes. For a moment it appeared as if the canoes were reflected in the woods across the river.

She looked down and shook her head, then looked back at the woods. "That's no illusion," she said aloud. "Come on, let's go."

She led the other four through the crowd,

weaving back and forth around the people. But she never took her eyes off the woods.

"What is it, Nancy?" George called from behind. Nancy could barely hear her over the chattering crowd.

"Look," Nancy pointed, nodding her head toward the woods.

"I see a light," Cory said. "It looks like a lantern in the woods."

"Oooh," Bess gasped. "The Lantern Lady?"

"Let's find out," Nancy said. "The footbridge is a few more yards down the river."

"That bridge is supposed to be dangerous," Amy warned. "Remember? During training, Mabel told us to stay off it."

"Some of the villagers told me they use it all the time," George said. "You just can't have a lot of people on it all at once. And you have to watch out for the holes and broken boards. The five of us should be okay. But we have to take it slowly."

"Just don't let anyone see us," Amy said. "We'll be in big trouble if Mabel finds out."

"No problem," Nancy said, leading them into the thick orchard. "You can't even see the bridge from here, and it's just on the other side of the orchard. Besides it's getting pretty dark, and everyone's watching the canoes—"

She was interrupted by a scream from the crowd behind them. Nancy looked across the

64

river. A cold shudder rippled through her as more screams and shouts filled the air.

On the far bank stood the figure of the Lantern Lady in a green hooded cloak with sleeves. From one arm dangled the lantern. The other arm was extended, its hand pointing straight at the canoes.

7

Watch Out, Nancy!

Nancy and the others watched the Lantern Lady on the far shore. The ghostly figure stood very still as she pointed at the parade of canoes.

"There she is!" shouted one of the tourists from the landing docks back at the village. Another screamed with fright.

"She's putting her jinx on the traders," yelled one of the villagers.

"Some of the people are laughing and clapping," Bess said.

"They probably think the Lantern Lady is part of the show," Cory pointed out. "I still think she is."

"Let's go find out," Nancy said. "Come on. The bridge isn't far."

Nancy ran ahead. The others followed close behind. They finally came to the footbridge. It was very old and definitely falling apart.

Nancy started across slowly. She held up the hem of her costume and petticoat so they wouldn't snag on the rotting boards. Bess, George, and Amy followed, carefully picking their way across the bridge. Cory waited a few minutes and then stepped onto the bridge.

"I can see why this is off-limits," George muttered. "And now I know why pioneer women wore such sturdy shoes."

"Just be careful," Bess warned. "Follow Nancy's lead."

Nancy stepped around the rotting boards. Every few feet she saw a dark opening where the wood had rotted or broken away. She could barely see the river, but she could hear it rushing beneath her. She wanted to hurry so she could get a closer look at the Lantern Lady, but she knew she had to be careful and that meant moving slowly.

Finally they all reached the other side and paused to catch their breath. The shadows of twilight were completely gone now. The almost-full moon was just rising. "There's the Lantern Lady," Nancy whispered, pointing to a spot ahead of them.

The figure seemed to be floating toward the

top of the hill ahead. They watched as her swinging light steadily climbed upward.

"I wish we had one of those lanterns," Nancy said. "Come on, let's keep moving after her." They carefully threaded their way through the trees and wild undergrowth pushing up from the floor of the thick, dark woods.

Some of the bushes had prickly brambles that snagged their costumes. Occasionally they had to stop to untangle their clothes from the sharp needles, but they also kept an eye on the fleeing figure.

Nancy constantly switched her gaze from the lantern flickering ahead to the floor of the woods. As she watched, the Lantern Lady's light went over the crest of the hill and out of view.

"Come on," Cory urged. "We've got to move or she's going to get away."

They climbed fast to the top of the hill, where Nancy stopped to get her bearings. They crouched behind a huge oak tree and looked down the other side of the hill. There were hardly any trees on that side—mostly just bushes and weeds. Moonlight bathed the landscape in a bright white glow. It was as if someone had covered the hill in a silky white veil.

"But where is she?" Amy whispered. "Where's the Lantern Lady?"

"Disappeared," Cory said, his voice hushed. "Back to the land of spirits. Oooooeeeeeoooooo."

"Stop that," Bess said. She turned to Nancy. "No kidding, where is she?"

Nancy continued looking around the side of the hill, squinting to focus. "I don't know," she said finally. "Cory's right. She's gone."

"That doesn't mean she's a ghost," George pointed out. "It could be anyone in a costume who just blew out the lantern."

"True," Nancy said. "And who's now crouched behind one of those bushes out of sight."

"Looking back up at us," Amy said in a tiny voice.

"Well, there's no sign of whoever it was," Nancy said with a sigh. "And our chances of finding her—or him—tonight are pretty slim. Actually, the Lantern Lady might even have doubled back toward the village."

"Sounds like a good idea to me," Bess said.

"I'm with you, cousin," George said.

They retraced their steps leading back to the Muskoka River. Halfway down the hill, Nancy noticed something clinging to the branch of a bush thick with brambles. "Look at this," she said.

Nancy held up a scrap of greenish white cloth

about the size of her palm. "Does this remind you of anything?" Nancy asked.

"Sure does," Cory said. "It looks like the Lantern Lady's cloak."

"Right," Nancy said. She kept looking at the piece of material.

"If that's true, then it's not a ghost," Bess concluded. "It's someone wearing a costume."

"But who?" Amy asked, staring at the material.

"Maybe Cory's right," George said. "Maybe it is part of the show here. They just don't tell anyone because it would ruin the legend."

"I don't know," Nancy said. "The Lantern Lady is getting some pretty bad publicity lately. People think she's responsible for the accidents and bad luck the village has had. I'm not sure that's the kind of publicity the village would make up."

"If it is someone in costume, I wonder who's playing the part?" Bess asked.

"It could be anybody," George said. "She's pretty far away when people see her. She wears this cloak that completely covers her. You can't see her size or shape—not even her shoes. She could just be walking, but because you can't see her feet, she appears to be floating. You can't even tell how tall she is really. You can't tell anything at all about what she looks like."

"She could even be a man," Nancy pointed out, frowning at the scrap of material.

"What is it, Nancy?" Cory asked. "What are you looking for?"

"I don't know," Nancy said. "It's just that there's something about this cloth. It reminds me of something else." Finally she tucked the scrap into her dress pocket. "Oh well, let's get back. It's getting late—probably nearly closing time."

Nancy was right. By the time they had crossed the rickety old bridge and wound their way back through the orchard, the village was closing. There were just a few straggling tourists left, who were being gently herded out by some of the villagers. Other villagers were tidying up, locking the buildings, and heading for the Visitors Center dressing rooms.

The Native Americans and voyageurs who had come to the village in canoes were setting up their tents in the meadow. Their campfires were sprinkled throughout the clearing, and the succulent aromas of roasting chicken and pork filled the air.

Nancy and the others hurried to their assigned work sites. When Nancy arrived at the doctor's house and office, it was already closed and locked. As she started back up the path to the Visitors Center, George ran out of the blacksmith's workshop.

71

"Nancy!" George called in a loud whisper. "Come here. Quick!"

Nancy followed George back up the path to the smithy's shop. As they neared the door, she could hear voices shouting in anger.

"You're taking this place into the ground, Jake," Nancy heard one voice yell.

"Don't tell me how to run my village," another voice shouted.

When Nancy and George rushed into the workshop, they saw two men facing each other. One was Jake Parrish. His fists were clenched, and his face was flushed with fury. The room had an orange-red glow from the flames of the blacksmith's fire. The light made Jake Parrish's red hair shine with bright highlights.

Nancy recognized the other man as the one Mabel had greeted—Leo Meier, the former director of the village and the man Jake Parrish had replaced a year ago. While Nancy and George watched, Parrish shoved Meier out of the way and started toward the doorway.

Meier rushed to the smithy's fire pit. Lying across the top of the pit was a long black iron rod. One end of the rod was pushed deep into the burning embers. The other end extended out so the blacksmith could grasp it.

Suddenly Meier grabbed the cool end of the

long rod with his left hand. Nancy checked his index finger. There was no ring.

Grasping the cool end, Meier pulled the rod out of the fire. The end of the rod that had been buried in the fire was white with a glowing red center. As he pulled, sparks flew through the air, showering Nancy and George. Instinctively, Nancy raised her arms to shield her face from the burning bits.

Waving the white-hot end of the rod, Meier turned and took a menacing step toward Parrish.

8

Where Did She Go?

Nancy's heart pounded as she watched Meier take another threatening step toward Parrish while waving the rod. The white-hot iron cut through the air like a glowing magician's wand.

"It's not my fault the village is in trouble," Parrish yelled at Meier. "It's yours! I've spent over a year just cleaning up the messes you left." He stood his ground, not flinching from the menacing Meier.

"Don't give me that," Meier responded. "You can't dump the blame on me. If we had put my ideas into motion, this would be the premier pioneer village attraction in the country."

Nancy decided she had to say something. But she didn't want to make the men more angry or have them turn their fury on her. She just wanted to calm them down so the argument wouldn't turn into a fight—or worse.

"Mr. Parrish," she said, smiling. "The village is closing. We need to lock up the shop."

The men ignored her. Nancy couldn't be positive they had even heard her.

"The premier pioneer attraction in the country!" Parrish yelled, repeating Meier's claim. "Ha! Not with you in charge. We lost money hand over fist when you were in charge, and you know it."

"At least it was an honest loss," Meier said.

"What's that supposed to mean?" Parrish asked, his eyes narrowing.

"Everyone knows about it," Meier said. "Your little scheme is unraveling. I heard the embezzling rumors clear over in Europe. You're trying to get the village closed so you and your family can sell it to that airport developer."

"Why you—" In spite of the threat of the glowing rod, Parrish took a step toward Meier. Nancy had never seen anyone so angry. Parrish's face was so red, it looked as if it would explode. He raised a clenched fist.

"Wait!" Nancy called, taking a small step from the doorway. "Please, Mr. Parrish. Mr. Meier. Maybe you could talk about this somewhere else.

The village is closed, and George needs to cover the fire and lock up the building."

Both men turned to the doorway. They seemed surprised to see Nancy and George standing there.

"Who are you?" Jake Parrish asked. "What are you doing here?"

"My name is Nancy Drew, and I'm one of the villagers in the doctor's house. This is George. She plays the smithy's daughter. She'd like to close up the workshop now."

Nancy knew that Jake Parrish, as the village director, could certainly take care of closing up the shop himself. But she hoped that by talking about a routine task she might distract the men enough to calm them down.

It seemed to be working. Leo Meier dropped his arm and let the rod clang to the floor, sparks flying as it landed. Parrish's fists relaxed a little, although he seemed to be keeping his guard up, just in case.

"You're not going to get away with it, Jake," Meier finally said, his voice still tight with anger. "I promise you that." He turned quickly and stormed to the door, brushing Nancy aside as he left.

Without a word, Jake Parrish followed him out and onto the path leading to the Visitors Center.

When Nancy looked out the door, Meier was already out of sight.

"You finish up here, George," Nancy said. "I want to talk to Mr. Parrish to see if I can find out anything more." She left the smithy's shop and ran up the path. The rows of tin lanterns flickering along both sides of the dark path helped light Nancy's way.

"Mr. Parrish," Nancy called.

Parrish stopped and turned. "Yes, what is it?" he asked. As Nancy expected, he appeared very rattled and angry from his confrontation with Meier. She knew she had to be very careful. If she added to his discomfort, she might lose her job in the village.

"I just thought I'd check to see if there was anything I could do," she said. "My friend and I were witnesses at the scene. We saw Mr. Meier threaten you. If you need us to speak with the police or anything . . ."

"No!" he said sharply. "There won't be any police involved." He seemed to force a small smile. "Thank you very much—Miss Drew, is it?" This time his voice was softer, more friendly. "I appreciate your concern. But it was merely a disagreement between former business associates. Nothing for you to be alarmed about."

"I just wanted to make sure," Nancy said,

smiling. "After all, he did accuse you of embezzling and trying to sabotage the village. He even said you wanted to shut it down and sell it. That's not possible, is it? It would be such a loss to the area." She purposely repeated the accusations so that she could watch Parrish's reaction.

In the lantern light, Nancy saw Parrish's expression change. The muscles at the side of his mouth tightened.

"That is absolutely *not* true," Parrish responded. "I strongly suggest that you and your friend put the whole thing out of your minds, Miss Drew. We have a festival to put on here. The tourists are counting on us." With that, he turned and stomped up the path toward the Visitors Center.

George caught up with Nancy on the path and asked what happened. Nancy told George about her conversation with Parrish as they continued up the path.

When they got to the dressing rooms, Bess was waiting for them. "What happened to you?" she asked. "I've been waiting here forever. Cory and Amy waited for a while, but they had to leave. We were afraid the Lantern Lady had gotten you."

While they changed, Nancy and George told Bess about the scene in the smithy's shop.

"So Meier was left-handed," Bess said. "Do you suppose he's the one who grabbed you in Anita's office?"

"He wasn't wearing a ring," George pointed out.

"Maybe he just didn't wear it today," Nancy said. "Who says he has to wear it every day?" She sighed. "You're right, though, George. Without the ring, he's just another left-handed man."

"He accused Jake Parrish of embezzling, though," George pointed out. "So he might have been in Anita's office looking for the same proof you were."

"That's right, George," Bess said. "Do you think he's the one who trashed the gallery and gift shop, Nancy?"

"I don't know," Nancy replied. "I'm not sure what his motive would be."

When she was dressed in her jeans and a T-shirt, Nancy reached into the pocket in her costume and pulled out the scrap of material they had found on the hill.

"If the Lantern Lady is a ghost, why is she wearing human clothing?" Nancy asked. "But if she's a person, where did she disappear to when she went over the hill?"

"What are you getting at?" George asked.

"If the Lantern Lady is a person, there must be

a hiding place of some kind on the other side of that hill," Nancy explained. "Someplace she—or he—ducked into."

"But there weren't any buildings that we could see," Bess said.

"The moonlight was really bright, Nancy," George added. "We didn't see anything."

"I know, but we were in a hurry," Nancy said. "We were tracking down this so-called ghost. We didn't know the terrain, so we had to watch our steps the whole way. And we didn't realize we should be watching for a hideout."

"We're going back, right?" George said with a groan. "I can tell by the way you're talking. We're going back over that bridge and up over that hill."

"Now?" Bess asked, her eyes wide. "What if we get caught?"

"We won't," Nancy assured her. "We'll be careful. Practically everyone's gone. Let's hide out in the rest room till we don't hear any more voices. Just one quick look around and we'll be out of here."

The three friends stayed until they heard someone call into the locker room area. "Everybody out?" the woman's voice said. "I'm locking up." After a few seconds they heard the light switch click, the lock turn, and the door close.

They peeked out of the rest room. The locker

room was dark, so they felt their way to the door. Nancy quietly turned the lock and opened the door a couple of inches. She peered out into the hall. No one was there.

The three friends stepped into the hall. George reached around, reset the lock, and quietly closed the locker room door. Then they quickly walked to the end of the hall and out the service door.

They were behind the Visitors Center, and no one was in sight. They raced through the village, past the meadow where the traders were camped, and into the orchard. Once again they carefully picked their way across the decrepit footbridge. On the other side of the river, they wove through the brambles and trees toward the top of the hill. This time the moon was high above them and shone brightly into the woods. Nancy pulled a small flashlight from her backpack.

As they reached a point halfway up the hill, Nancy heard a noise behind them. She reached out and grabbed Bess and George, pulling them to a halt. She put her index finger to her lips and flicked off her flashlight.

The three stood there, straining to hear the sound again. Finally Nancy heard it again—a sharp crackling noise as if a twig or branch was breaking. Bess gasped and stood stone still.

George pointed down the hill to the spot where the noise had come from.

Nancy led her friends behind a tree. They ducked down and waited as the faint crackling noises became louder. Now it definitely sounded like footsteps coming up the hill behind them.

Nancy's breath came quickly. A chill washed over her as she focused on the sound. Something was following them, but what? Was it the night guard? Or a wild animal? She remembered hearing the villagers tell of coyotes in these woods.

Or have the tables been turned, Nancy wondered. Is the ghost of the Lantern Lady following us?

9

Disaster at Windbreak

Nancy held her breath as the footfalls moved closer. Then the dark floor of the woods was broken by the beam of a large flashlight. The light swung around until it caught Nancy, Bess, and George in its beam.

"What are you doing here?" a voice boomed at them.

Nancy couldn't see who it was because the light was in her eyes. But she recognized the voice, and her heart sank. It was Jake Parrish.

"Hi, Mr. Parrish," she said, stepping from behind the tree. "It's Nancy Drew."

"I repeat—what are you doing?" He looked at George. "I recognize you from the village," he said. "I saw you earlier in the blacksmith's shop, right?"

"Yes, sir, that's right," George answered.

"And who's this?" he asked, waving the beam of light at Bess.

"I'm Bess, sir. I'm one of the villagers working at Windbreak."

"All right," Parrish said. "Now, which one of you is going to tell me what's going on?"

Nancy thought fast. She was afraid that if she told the truth, they might lose their jobs. If she was no longer working there, her investigation into the strange events at Persimmon Woods would be over.

"I've lost a sweatshirt," she told him. "I thought I might have left it up here. Some of us did some exploring on this side of the river during a break in our training session last weekend. I talked Bess and George into hiking up here with me to see if we could find it."

"This is an odd time of day to be doing that, don't you think?" he said, his eyes narrowing as he studied her face.

Nancy took a deep breath. She wasn't sure Parrish believed her. "Well, yes," she answered, "but we're so busy during the day, I couldn't find time. Besides, it would have been so much harder in our costumes."

"Don't you know how dangerous these woods

are?" Parrish said. "Especially at night. There are coyotes—and snakes. Dropoffs and tree roots are hidden under the leaves. Not to mention some of the crazy unexplained things that have been happening around here. You could have been hurt."

"You're right, of course," Nancy said. "This is not a good time to be prowling around in the woods. It's late and we really should be going home. Come on, girls."

She turned quickly and started down the hill, followed by George and Bess. She hoped Parrish would just let them go. But then she heard his voice saying loudly, "Wait a minute!"

She turned back and smiled, saying, "Mr. Parrish, I'm really sorry. We shouldn't have come up here so late." Then she looked him squarely in the eye and added, "We would have come up here earlier, but George was late locking up the blacksmith's shop."

She knew she had made her point when she saw his eyebrow tilt upward. It was if she had sent him a coded message. You asked me to forget the scene between you and Leo Meier, she was hinting. I'm asking you to forget that you found us up here after hours.

Parrish's expression softened a little, and he nodded his head. "Okay, let's go down to the village. I'll walk you to your car."

Nancy and her friends went back down the hill, followed by Jake Parrish. No one said a word during the trek back. In fifteen minutes they were in the parking lot next to Nancy's Mustang.

Bess and George got into the car, but Nancy turned at her door. "Mr. Parrish," she said, "you're right. There have been a lot of strange things going on around here. What do you think is causing it? Is someone trying to ruin Persimmon Woods Pioneer Village?"

In the harsh light of the security lamp bulb, Nancy could see Parrish's face return to the dark angry red she had seen in the smithy's workshop. "You were hired to interpret pioneer life for the tourists, Miss Drew," he said in a low voice. "I suggest you stick to that and leave the problems and concerns of the village to me."

He turned abruptly and stalked over to his car. By the time Nancy had started up her engine, Parrish had peeled out of the parking lot, flinging gravel up from the tires of his dark blue luxury sedan.

"We've just got to spend the night soon at the village," Nancy said to Bess and George as she drove them home.

"What!" George said. "After all we went through tonight? I'm not too thrilled about even working there during the daytime now."

"I think it's getting exciting," Bess said.

"Nancy's right. We could really poke around if we were alone out there."

"What are we going to look for exactly?" George asked.

"I still want to see whether there's a hideout on the other side of the hill that the Lantern Lady uses," Nancy said. "I also want to get back into the offices and see whether we can find any evidence of embezzling."

"We could hide out in the loft of the blacksmith's cabin," George said. "It's closed off to tourists, and no one ever goes up there. It's just got extra furniture and junk in it. I have the key to let us in."

"Good," Nancy said. "And then we'll have free rein to explore all we want."

"And we stay up there till no one's left in the village this time, right?" Bess asked.

"No one except the Lantern Lady, of course," George said with a smile.

Wednesday morning was clear and beautiful. Nancy reported to work at the doctor's house and was met by Mabel Tansy.

"Good morning," Mabel said. "I have a treat for you. We need someone to fill in at Windbreak, and since you're the floater, you'll be moving over there today. I'll walk you over and get you started."

As they walked down the path to the large brick home of the village founder, Nancy decided to ask Mabel a few questions. "After I got home I realized who Leo Meier was," she said. "That man you greeted yesterday."

"Really?" Mabel said.

"Yes," Nancy said. "He and Mr. Parrish had a big falling out, didn't they? Mr. Meier was fired, and there was even a lawsuit."

"Yes," Mabel said. "I believe you're right."

"I wonder what Mr. Meier was doing here," Nancy said. "I wouldn't think Mr. Parrish would want him hanging around the village. Or that Mr. Meier would want to."

"I don't know anything about that, Nancy," Mabel said. "I haven't talked to either one about it. Well, now, here we are."

They walked into the large kitchen at the back of Windbreak. Bess was getting out some of the vegetables they would be cleaning and cooking for the noon meal.

"Nancy!" Bess called when they walked in. "Are you filling in here today?"

"Yes, she is," Mabel said, bustling around the room to check that everything was in its place. "Where's Cory?"

"I don't know," Bess answered. "I talked to Amy earlier. She said Cory was still in the dressing room when she left. I'm sure he'll be along in a little while."

"He'd better be," Mabel said. "We open soon. Well, carry on." She bustled out the door.

"This is going to be great," Bess said, as she and Nancy walked into the parlor to await the first batch of tourists. "This house is so cool," Bess said. "You'll love working here. There's someone upstairs to show the tourists the bedrooms. You and I will walk them through the downstairs."

By the afternoon Nancy and Bess had escorted dozens of tourist groups, and it had become a comfortable routine. Tourists entered the parlor in small groups. Bess pointed out the fine furniture, including Brandon Parrish's desk, which he brought into the house in the 1830s. The parlor also had a children's corner, with small furniture, wooden toys, and board games.

From the parlor Nancy led the group into the dining room. The table was set for twelve. A beautiful embroidered tablecloth was covered with painted china and pale gold glassware. A large sideboard against the wall held silver dishes and pewter trays ready to be filled.

Then Bess led the group into the kitchen and over to the large fireplace. There, she and Nancy demonstrated the cooking. First, Nancy showed them the huge iron kettle swinging over the fire. She lifted the lid and the smell of beef stew filled the kitchen.

Then she took a long hook and pulled a pan out from under the coals at the bottom of the fire. "This is called a spider pan," she said. "You can see why." She pointed to the bottom of the pan and the long legs that held it up off the fireplace floor. She removed the lid to show the bubbling golden crust of an apple cobbler.

Then Bess took over. "We're right proud of this next contraption," she said, using the dialect words they had learned in their training. "We're the only village hereabouts to have them. We have one here, and I hear Dr. Herman has one, too."

Bess explained how the chain-turned spit worked, winding the wheel and turning the golden roasting chicken. "It's a modern miracle," she said, grinning. Her eyes sparkled as she spoke.

Nancy gazed out the window. Even after hearing it so many times, she enjoyed listening. Bess was wonderful in her part. Her natural acting ability and bubbly personality made her a hit with the tourists.

"Finally, we come to the beehive oven," Bess continued, pointing to the door in the brick wall. "You probably noticed the round brick dome outside. That hood holds in the heat and releases it slowly through air vents. We cook delicious bread and cakes in it. It holds several loaves at a time."

As Bess spoke, something outside caught Nancy's eye. She saw someone run quickly from the house into a small cornfield.

"As you can see," Bess continued, reaching for the beehive oven door, "it's very large and holds—"

"Oh, no!" one of the tourists gasped in a mock scream. Nancy jumped and her attention jolted instantly back to the kitchen. She looked at the open beehive oven door. Cory Worth's face stared out at everyone, his eyes sparkling with mischief. He was crouched on his stomach on the floor of the oven, his arms tucked under his chest, with an apple in his grinning mouth.

The startled scream of the tourist changed to giggles. Bess kept her poise and continued speaking. "As you can see, we pioneers often cook strange things."

Nancy's surprised laugh joined with the others as Bess calmly closed the door again and tripped the small latch that locked it shut. Nancy's laugh caught in her throat as she heard other screams, this time from upstairs. "Help!" someone yelled. "It's burning! Please help us. Fire!"

10

A Golden Clue

"Fire!" yelled another voice from the second floor of Windbreak. "The house is on fire!"

Nancy raced to the stairs. The tour group from the second floor was pounding down the wooden steps. Some people were panicking and were trying to shove their way to the front of the line. This caused others to stumble and trip down the steep old stairs.

"Please, everyone," Nancy called over the screams. "It's just a short way to the doors. Everyone will be fine."

Some seemed to be calmed by her words and slowed their frantic pace. Others continued yelling as they lurched madly for the doors, jamming up against the downstairs tour group.

Nancy was joined by the villager who had led the tour group. She could hear the fire popping and crackling upstairs. The smell of smoke and charred wood began to fill the hallway. As she guided the flustered tourists down the hall, she saw flames begin to lick the parlor ceiling.

Nancy's heart jumped a beat when she saw a small girl starting to tumble to the floor at the bottom of the steps. "Please!" Nancy called again. "Just calm yourselves and watch out for the children."

She scooped up the little girl and raced outdoors. "Bess!" Nancy yelled over her shoulder. "Get help!"

"She already left to call the firefighters," one of the tourists in Nancy's group said as he followed her out with another child. They handed the children over to several full-time villagers who had gathered outside Windbreak. Within minutes, the parents swooped over and gathered their children in their arms.

"George!" Nancy said as she saw her friend run over the lawn from the smithy's cabin. "I'm glad you're here. Help me get everyone away from the house." As she spoke, she heard *pop, pop, pop* behind her. The crowd watched as, one by one, the antique windows with the wavy glass began exploding.

"The firefighters are on the way," Bess assured

the crowd as she ran up. Then she ran to Nancy and George. "It's a volunteer fire department," she said, panting because she was out of breath. "But they said they'd be here in just a few minutes."

"Nancy!" Bess called. "What about Cory? Did you see him? Did he get out?"

Nancy felt a stab of horror. Cory! She had been so busy with the tourists and the little girl, she had completely forgotten him. Unless someone else had slipped the oven door latch, he was still locked in the beehive. She and Bess raced around to the kitchen door. It was on the far side of the house, away from the fire in the parlor.

They heard Cory's muffled yells when they ran into the kitchen. The beehive oven was right next to the door. Quickly Bess lifted the latch and Cory scrambled out. His eyes were wide with fright, but he managed a smile. "I knew you'd come," he said, panting. "I just wasn't sure when."

The three stepped out of the door and circled to the front. "You two stay with the crowd," Nancy said. "I'll be right back."

Nancy walked cautiously around the perimeter of the house, looking for clues as to what might have happened.

As she searched, she noticed a dark, narrow streak in the grass. It was a few yards long and led away from the front corner of the house. She bent down and touched the streak. It was ashy and still warm. As she walked along the charred path, parts of it were still smoking.

Nancy guessed that someone had poured something flammable along this trail. Then the arsonist had set it on fire at the far end. As the flames burned the flammable substance, they traveled up to the house and then set it on fire.

Nancy followed the trail away from the house to the cornfield. She remembered the person she had seen running in this same direction while Bess talked to the tourists in the kitchen. That had happened just before the fire broke out.

Nancy cautiously followed the same path. She looked around but saw no sign of anyone in the cornfield. Frustrated, she looked back at the house. The crowd was parting to let the firefighters through.

By this time the parlor side of Windbreak was engulfed in flames. The bricks on the outside were black, and fire flared out of the paneless windows.

Guards were pushing the crowd back away from the house. Water began gushing from the firehoses. Nancy looked more closely at the ground in the cornfield, especially the area where she had seen the person disappear.

She was sure it was no coincidence that someone ran away from Windbreak just before it caught fire, especially since she had discovered the smoking trail.

She thought of the terrified people scrambling down the stairs to escape the flames. She got chills when she remembered the little girl tumbling into danger and Cory locked in the beehive oven. She was more determined than ever to find something—anything—that would help her figure out what happened.

She got on her knees and began gently examining the undergrowth, hoping to find a clue. But there was nothing.

She left the cornfield and walked along the charred streak in the lawn, checking from side to side. There! What was that? Something shiny caught her eye. It glinted at her from a clump of weeds a foot from the still-smoking trail.

She picked it up, and for a moment she held her breath. It was a gold ring with an unusual scroll pattern. Inside the ring were etched the initials L. M.

Nancy released her held breath with a whoosh. She rushed around to the front of the house where Bess, George, Cory, and Amy were standing and led them away from the crowd.

"First of all," Nancy said, "is everyone all right? Cory, are you okay?" Nancy asked.

"Sure," he answered. He held up his hands.

Some of his knuckles were scraped and red. "I lost a little skin banging on the oven door, but other than that I'm okay."

"Maybe that will teach you to stop taking such chances," Amy told him. "Someday you're going to trick your way into a real jam."

"Easy, little sis," he said with a lopsided grin. "I told you I'm okay."

"That must have been some sight," George said.

"I can't believe how calm Bess was when she opened the door the first time," Nancy added. "She didn't even flinch."

"That's because he'd done it before," Bess told the others. "Believe me, the first time he pulled that, I jumped plenty."

"And screamed," Cory said, giving her a playful hug.

"Everyone else seems to be fine," George told Nancy. "Everyone got out of the fire with no injuries."

"Good," Nancy said with a deep breath.

"Where did you go?" Cory asked.

"I did a little snooping," Nancy answered. Quickly she told them about the person she had seen from the kitchen window. Then she described the charred trail leading from the cornfield to Windbreak. Finally she showed them the ring she had found.

97

"L. M.," Bess said.

"Leo Meier?" George whispered.

"Right!" Nancy said. "What's more, I'm sure he's the one who attacked me. Remember? I could tell he was left-handed because the first thing he did was grab my mouth with his left hand. And I looked down and saw that he was wearing a ring on his index finger."

"I remember you told us that the ring had a scroll pattern on it," Amy added.

"Look," Nancy said, holding up the ring.

"There's a pattern, all right," Cory said. "But who's Leo Meier?"

"Bess. Cory," Mabel called from the lawn in front of Windbreak. "I need you to help us clear out the visitors."

Nancy dropped the ring in her pocket. "I'll tell you all about him later," she said. "For now, you and Bess go help Mabel."

Cory nodded, then grabbed Bess's hand. Together, they ran to join Mabel.

Nancy turned to Amy and George. "You two come with me," she said. "Three sets of eyes are better than one. Maybe we can find something else."

She led George and Amy around the general store, behind the barn, and into the back of the small cornfield. They walked through it, looking for more clues. But they found nothing.

They stood at the edge of the cornfield and looked toward Windbreak. "I think the fire is out," Amy said.

As they watched, the firefighters brought the ruined furniture and rugs out onto the lawn surrounding the house.

"It doesn't look like we're going to find anything more here," Nancy said. "Let's go back and—"

"Don't move," said a menacing voice from behind. "Don't even turn around."

11

But Is It Really Over?

"Do what he says," Nancy whispered to George and Amy standing next to her in the cornfield.

"Just don't move," the man said behind them. "I am armed. I don't want to hurt you. I just want something back."

Nancy's heart was pounding in her temples. "What is it?" she asked.

"I believe you have something that belongs to me," the man said. "I saw you pick something up off the lawn a little while ago. Throw it back here and you won't be hurt."

"Do you mean this?" she asked, holding up the ring.

"Yes," the man said. "That's it. I must have

dropped it earlier. When I retraced my steps to find it, I saw you pick it up."

"You say you retraced your steps," Nancy said. "Do you mean the steps you took to set the fire at Windbreak? I found your ring near where the fire was started."

The man was silent for a moment. "Just throw it back here," he finally said. "Then count to twenty, and go on about your business."

"That won't work," Nancy said. "There are so many people here, you'll never get away without being seen. My whole tour group saw you from the kitchen of Windbreak," she added, stretching the truth. "We saw you run from the house into this cornfield just before the fire started."

"That's right," George said, joining in. "We all can describe you to the police and the fire marshal. And Nancy showed the ring to a lot of the people," George added. "They can describe it—and the initials inside."

The man behind them gasped.

"Harming us won't help you escape justice," Nancy said in a low voice. "You might as well let us go." Time seemed to pass very slowly. She could hear the crowd at Windbreak, but they seemed very far away. Her senses were tuned sharply to what was going on behind her.

Finally, after what seemed like minutes—but was probably only seconds—she heard footsteps behind her, running away from them. Nancy turned to see the man racing from the cornfield. He stopped and leaned against the barn. His shoulders slumped and he rubbed his eyes with his left hand. He was too far away to identify positively, but Nancy was sure it was Leo Meier.

Nancy, George, and Amy returned to the crowd at Windbreak. George stayed with Cory, Amy, and the other villagers trying to get the tourists to leave. Nancy and Bess sought out the fire marshal and told him they had been working in Windbreak when the fire broke out.

The fire marshal asked Nancy and Bess many questions about what they had seen and heard. Jake Parrish joined the group briefly. "You again?" he said to Nancy. "You really do have a talent for being in the thick of things, don't you?" He stayed and listened for a few minutes, then went inside Windbreak.

Nancy showed the fire marshal the charred trail leading to the house. "We had already discovered that, miss," he said. "And we agree that it looks very suspicious."

Then Nancy handed the fire marshal the ring she had found. She told him about the threatening encounter with the man in the cornfield. "I'm not sure who it was," Nancy said. "But I think it was Leo Meier."

*   *   *

Nancy and Bess rejoined George, Cory, Amy, Mabel, and the other villagers. Jake Parrish insisted on keeping the village open until regular closing time. George returned to the smithy's cabin and Amy to the general store.

Most of the tourists had left the area and were continuing their visit through the rest of the village. Mabel asked Nancy, Bess, and Cory to take positions in the perimeter paths around Windbreak. They spent the rest of the day steering visitors away from the big brick home and into the rest of the village.

When the workday finally ended, Nancy, Bess, and George headed to the Drews' for well-deserved pizzas. When they arrived at the house, Hannah met them at the door. "Hurry," she said, bustling back into the living room. "They're talking about the fire on the news."

Nancy ordered their pizza as they watched the news broadcast. The local anchor talked about the day's excitement at the woods.

"Former Persimmon Woods Pioneer Village director Leo Meier has confessed to arson," the woman said. "He admits setting the fire that destroyed half of Windbreak, the original home of Brandon Parrish in the historic settlement."

"Wow!" Bess said. "He really did it. He confessed!"

"Shhhh," George said. "I want to hear the rest."

"Local citizens will recall the trouble a year ago between Meier and the current director, Jake Parrish, who is a descendant of the founder," the anchor continued. "Field reporter Ron Edward has exclusive interviews with both men. Ron?"

"Thanks, Rose," the reporter said. "Meier talked with me from jail after his arraignment at the courthouse." The TV picture changed to a shot of a small room with two men sitting in wooden chairs.

"There he is," Bess said. "There's Leo Meier."

"You worked at Persimmon Woods for years," the reporter said. "You put your heart and energy into the place. Today you set fire to its most important building. Only one question: why?"

"I had to get back at that crook Jake Parrish, that's why," Meier said, his face pale. He then went into a rambling statement about how he had been forced out of his job and had had to abandon his lawsuit. "I just couldn't see any other way to make Parrish suffer," he said, shaking his head as he slumped forward in his chair.

"So you cooked up all these nasty accidents and calamities for the village?" the reporter concluded.

"No!" Meier said. "Just the fire. I'm not to

blame for anything else that's happened out there. Just the fire today. I'd heard about the rest of it, of course. In fact, that's what made me think I could get away with the fire. I figured everyone would think it was just the latest disaster. Unfortunately, someone saw me and put together some other clues—"

"Nancy!" Bess said. "He's talking about you!"

"So that's why you confessed?" the reporter asked. "Because you knew they were going to catch you anyway?"

"That's part of it," Meier said. "I have to admit that. But I also confessed because what I did was awful. And it could have been a lot worse. I'm thankful no one was hurt." He looked directly into the camera. Nancy wondered whether he was telling the truth.

"Anyway," Meier finished. "I didn't do anything to harm the village except set the fire. I've been in Europe for a year. I wasn't even in the country when those other things happened."

The camera zoomed to a closeup of Ron Edward's face. "Well, that's Meier's story," the reporter said. "But there's one person who doesn't believe it for a minute."

The television picture changed to the reception area in the Visitors Center at the village. Reporter Ron Edward was now speaking with

105

Jake Parrish. "I don't believe a thing Meier says," Jake said. "He did everything he could in the past to destroy this place. Setting fire to Windbreak was more extreme but just part of his pattern. He's guilty of more than just the fire. I'm sure of that."

Once again the camera zoomed in to a closeup of Ron Edward. "Well, folks, we know who set the fire today, but we still aren't sure who was responsible for the other incidents. The police will have to determine that. Is Meier innocent of the previous village problems? Then who is the culprit? Perhaps we can lay the blame at the feet of the Lantern Lady after all. Back to you, Rose."

Nancy turned off the television set so she and her friends could talk while they waited for the pizza.

"Well, what do you think, Nancy?" George asked. "Is Leo Meier behind all the rest of the trouble at Persimmon Woods?"

"I don't know," Nancy said. "He says he was in Europe until recently. If that's true, it should be pretty easy to check."

"But if he didn't cause all the other problems at the village, then we're back to our same old questions," Bess said. "Who did—and why?"

"Nancy, you do think Leo Meier is the one who grabbed you, don't you?" George asked.

106

"Yes, definitely," Nancy answered.

"But if someone *is* embezzling," Bess said, "it really couldn't be Leo Meier. He'd have no way of getting to the money." She studied Nancy. "This case isn't over yet, is it?" she said.

"Even if Leo Meier did everything to cause the accidents and other problems in the village," George added, "that doesn't really explain the embezzling. There's definitely something else going on."

"That's right," Nancy said. "And what if Leo Meier can prove he's innocent of all the rest of it except the fire. That means there's still some nut out there trying to close the village down."

"Who do you think it is?" Bess asked.

"I don't really know," Nancy said. "If we could just pin down a motive, we might figure out the answer."

The doorbell interrupted them. "Pizza!" George and Bess said simultaneously.

When Nancy opened the door, she was met by both the delivery man and her father, who was paying for the pizzas. Over her father's shoulder, she was surprised to see a small drive-it-yourself moving truck pull into Anita's driveway. Anita got out and went into her house.

Carson Drew carried in the pizzas. "I heard about the fire over the radio while I drove home," he said. "And I can't wait to hear about it from your point of view. But I've got some news of my own first."

He put the pizzas on the kitchen table. "Anita Valdez is moving. My associate told me she's way behind on her mortgage payments and deep in debt. The bank's foreclosing on her house."

12

The Hidden Observers

"Anita's moving?" Nancy said.

"Because she's badly in debt?" Bess echoed. "Nancy! You were just saying you needed a motive to pin down the embezzler."

"Oh, I can't believe it's Anita, though," Nancy said. "She's the one who asked me to investigate in the first place."

"You're right," Bess said. "That doesn't make any sense. If she *was* the embezzler, she wouldn't ask you to investigate the embezzling."

"Unless she's trying to throw you off the track somehow," George said.

"Come on," Bess said. "Anita is Nancy's friend."

"I know it," George said. "I'm not saying she's

109

guilty. But Jake Parrish seems to think so. I'm just trying to think of all the possibilities, the way a good detective does. Right, Nancy?"

"Ummm, right," Nancy mumbled. "You guys go ahead and eat. I'll be right back."

She ran across the lawn to Anita's house and knocked on the door. There was no answer. She knocked again, but still no one came to the door. With a sigh, Nancy turned and went back home.

"I tried to talk to her," she said when she rejoined the others around the kitchen table. "But she didn't answer my knock."

"That's strange," Carson said. "I saw her drive in earlier."

"I did, too," Nancy added as she reached for a piece of pizza.

"Maybe she left again and you just didn't see her," Bess offered.

"Mmmmm," Nancy said. "Maybe."

"So let me see if I have this straight," George said. "Anita accuses Jake of embezzling. But Jake fires her, accusing *her* of embezzling. Obviously, something's going on with the foundation's money. But which one is guilty?"

"Not Anita," Bess said. "Right, Nancy?"

"I hope not," Nancy said.

When the pizza was gone, George stretched, saying, "We may still have a lot of questions about what's been happening at the village. But I've learned one thing for certain—they sure worked hard in those days."

"You know, I was thinking about that earlier," Bess said. "Just imagine going through that fire in the 1830s. No nine-one-one calls, no fancy fire trucks. It would have been awful."

"It sure would," George said, standing up. "And on that note, I'm sorry to say I need to get home. Are you ready to go, Bess?"

"Let's help Nancy clean up first," Bess said. "Then we'll go."

"I'm glad you drove over here this morning, George," Nancy said as the three cleared the table. "Now I don't have to go back out again."

"No problem," George said. "I'll do it again tomorrow morning. Boy, I'm really tired. That bed's going to feel good tonight."

Nancy walked her friends to George's car. They looked over at Anita's house. The moving truck and her car were both in the driveway, and a light was on in the living room.

"Okay," Nancy said while George started the car. "Tomorrow night we stay over at the village. We'll hide out in the loft of the blacksmith's cabin till everyone's gone. Then we'll go back into Anita's office."

"If we wait until everyone's gone, the building will be locked," George said. "How do we get in?"

"I've checked out the service door lock," Nancy said. "I think I can manage it."

"Do you think there's any evidence left in the office records by now?" Bess asked. "With all this publicity since the fire, whoever's doing the embezzling may have destroyed the records."

"Could be," Nancy said. "But I have to check to make sure. And let's not mention any of this to Cory and Amy," she added. "I think three's enough for this adventure."

"Good idea," George said, starting up her car. "See you in the morning."

After her friends left, Nancy tried knocking on Anita's door again. There still was no answer. When Nancy got back inside her own house, she phoned. Anita answered but told Nancy she didn't want to talk to anyone.

Thursday morning George drove to the Drews'. Nancy told her father what they were planning that evening. Then she drove Bess and George out to the village. When they arrived, she by-passed the employee parking lot and eased the Mustang behind two tractors in back of the maintenance shed. She figured the car wouldn't be noticed there when everyone left.

It was a busier day than the previous three. There were even more people than on opening day. Mabel reasoned that it was because of the fire. "Any kind of excitement brings out the curiosity seekers," she said. "Even disasters."

"Were you surprised that Leo Meier confessed to the fire?" Nancy asked.

"Surprised!" Mabel repeated. "Shocked is more like it. Hard to believe, hard to believe. And such a nice man, too. Oh well, you never know, I guess."

Windbreak was closed, of course. Bess and Cory were designated floaters for the rest of the week, along with Nancy. Cory was sent to the potter's cabin. Nancy and Bess were assigned to help Amy in the general store. It was kind of a crazy day. The tourists seemed just as interested in what the villagers thought about the fire as they were in pioneer life.

At noon Cory came by the store with a picnic. He and Amy, Bess, George, and Nancy sat on the lawn outside the store and ate cold chicken, fruit, and muffins.

"The potter's cabin is pretty cool," Cory said. "But it's hard work. The potter turns the pitchers, mugs, and bowls on the wheel all day. But I'm the guy who has to carry them all out to the kiln in back."

"How many have you broken so far?" Amy asked.

"None, smartie," Cory said. He cut a pear in two and gave half to Bess.

"I don't believe it," Amy said. "At home you break a dish or plate at least once or twice a week."

"It's all a plot, sister dear," Cory said. "I figure if I break enough, I'll get out of kitchen duty forever."

Amy threw a muffin at Cory. He caught it expertly, broke it in two, and handed half to Bess. Nancy, Amy, and George exchanged grins, but Cory and Bess didn't seem to notice.

Everyone breathed a sigh of relief when the day ended without a major disaster or an appearance by the Lantern Lady.

Amy and Cory left immediately for a family get-together. After changing into their jeans and sweaters, Nancy, Bess, and George grabbed their backpacks and headed for the woods behind the blacksmith's cabin. They hid out there until they saw the blacksmith and his wife leave and lock the cabin and workshop doors.

George led Nancy and Bess to the back door of the cabin. She let them in with her key, and the three hurried up the steps to the cabin loft. It had a dusty wooden floor and a few pieces of furniture scattered around.

It was very dark up there except for the places between the logs where light leaked through. In one of those spots, the chinking that plastered the logs together had crumbled away. It left an opening about two inches high and six inches long. Nancy sat on the old floor and watched the rest of the village through that opening.

In the distance to the left, she could see the meadow where the traders and their families were camped. Many of them were settling down to their evening meal. To the right beyond the village, she could see the parking lot. She had a perfect spot to watch and wait.

Within an hour it was quiet on the paths. The sun had gone down and the village was full of shadows. The lanterns lining the paths were still flickering. Soon, as Nancy watched, the night guard came by and extinguished them all with a water pistol aimed perfectly through the star-shaped openings that had been cut in the tops of the lanterns.

Nancy watched as the guard started toward the Visitors Center. Then he stopped and turned back. As she followed him with her eyes, the guard walked back down the path past the smithy's cabin and disappeared from view.

"Now, where do you suppose he's going," Nancy wondered. She told Bess and George what she had seen. She continued her vigil, although the view became dimmer and dimmer as night fell. "Wait!" she exclaimed. "There he is again. I see him."

George and Bess crowded in to see what Nancy

reported. The guard had gone into the meadow to the traders' camp.

"Maybe he wants to buy something," George said.

"Perhaps he's just lonely," Bess suggested. "Or hungry. Someone's bound to offer him something to eat."

"Speaking of which," George said. "I could use a little something myself. There's a plate of cookies on the table downstairs. They're left from our noon meal."

"Look," Nancy said. "This is a perfect time to go to the Visitors Center. The parking lot is clear. All the villagers and staff must be gone."

"Best of all, the guard's not there," Bess added.

"And probably won't be for a while," Nancy said, standing up. "He just sat down to a large platter of food with some of the traders who are camping out there. Let's go!"

The three clambered down the stairs, grabbed some cookies, and peered out the cabin door. There was no one in sight. Quickly, dodging from tree to tree and building to building, they made their way to the Visitors Center, munching cookies along the way.

Nancy and her lock-pick got them in the service door with no problem. She led Bess and George quickly up the back stairway to the administration offices. Nancy stopped at the rest room where she had gotten the chair the last time she had been there. The chair was still there.

She stopped in front of Anita's office, stepped on the chair, and opened the transom window. Then she crawled through and dropped to the floor inside the office. Bess and George followed her lead.

Nancy turned on the desk light, and they quickly went to work. "Bess, see what you can find on the computer," Nancy said. "George, you and I can check the file cabinet and desk."

Bess opened the computer and scanned the databases, but found nothing that looked like embezzlement evidence. Nancy and George found a few receipts and order vouchers that might indicate something, but they weren't sure.

"Let's copy them, just in case," George said, taking them to the copy machine in the corner of the office.

As she started the machine, Nancy thought she heard a faint scratching noise out in the hall. With a jolt, she remembered her last experience in this room. She could still feel the harsh grip of Leo Meier's hand over her mouth as she was dragged into the loft.

"Stop the copier," she whispered, reaching to turn off the desk light. "Listen!"

13

The Lantern Lady's Lair

When Nancy heard the scratching noise out in the hall the second time, a shudder fluttered down her back. The memory of the last time she was here flooded over her, and her body jumped into action. "Follow me," she whispered. She grabbed the files from George and forced them back into the cabinet. George shut off the copier, Bess turned off the computer, and they followed Nancy out the back door of the office.

The room was very dark, but Nancy knew where she was. When she'd been trapped there before, a thin stream of sunlight barely shone through the dirty window. This time it was a ray of moonlight. Nancy could barely see, but she knew she was in the same loft over the storeroom that she had been shoved into the last time. She could tell by the musty, dusty smell.

"Where are we?" Bess whispered. Nancy could hear a nervous flutter in her friend's voice. "Is this where Leo Meier shoved you in the closet?"

"That's right," Nancy said, her voice hushed, nodding toward the closet door. She didn't want to turn on her flashlight. She stayed still until she could get her bearings in the dark room. "Get down and don't move," she added. "We're in a loft, remember? I don't want anyone falling over the railing into the storeroom below."

They all crouched on the floor. Nancy put her ear next to the closed door of Anita's old office. She heard nothing. Carefully, she eased the door open a few inches. With a sudden whoosh, a field mouse scampered through the opening and disappeared under a box.

"Yikes!" Bess exclaimed. "Where did *that* come from?" She jumped to her feet and stepped away from the wall.

"The mouse must have been what we heard scratching earlier," Nancy said, relaxing a little. But her senses stayed alert to anything that might put them in danger. "I don't hear anything more," she whispered. "But let's get out of here, just in case."

She flicked on her flashlight. They walked

along the loft railing, then climbed down the stairs to the storeroom behind the museum gallery.

As they walked through the storeroom, Bess stopped to look at an old map. It was about two feet square and had been drawn by hand in pen and ink. It was in a simple frame and propped against the wall.

"Look," Bess said sadly, pointing to a spot on the map. "There's Windbreak."

"And there's the smithy's cabin and shop," George added.

"I don't see the doctor's house," Nancy said. "This map must have been made before the doctor's family came to the village."

"Here's something that's not here any longer," George pointed out. "An icehouse."

"You're right," Nancy said. "It's not in the village, though. It's across the river. And this shows there's a house there, too." They all studied the map.

"Nancy," George said, her eyes wide with discovery.

"Right, George," Nancy said. She knew what her friend was thinking. "Both buildings are located on the other side of the hill—where the Lantern Lady disappeared."

"Oh, Nancy, do you think something's still there?" Bess asked.

"Could be," Nancy said. "If there's an old structure there, it might be in terrible shape. It could have looked like part of the undergrowth to us in the moonlight."

"But someone could still duck into it and hide," George added.

"Exactly!" Nancy said. "Let's get out there—now."

The three crossed the storeroom to the huge sliding pocket door that led to the museum gallery. Nancy was about to push the button to open the door, when she heard a crash behind her.

"Oooh," George moaned. "Oh, no." Nancy and Bess rushed back to where George lay. "I tripped over that footstool," she said. "I think I've twisted my ankle."

"Can you stand?" Bess asked, helping her up.

"Yeah, yeah, I'm okay," George said. Nancy could tell her friend was hurting, but George insisted they get out of the Visitors Center and head for the hill.

Nancy pushed the button opening the pocket door, and they stepped into the gallery. Then she tapped the candle sconce to close the door behind them. They tiptoed through the gallery and out the door, locking it behind them. No one was in the Visitors Center reception area, so they headed down the hall as quickly as possible to the service door.

121

George limped along, but it was clear she would never make it over the old bridge and up the hill through the woods. She finally sat down on a stump for a rest. "I'm just going to slow you two down," she said. "You go ahead. I'll stay in the smithy's cabin until you get back. Come around to the back door and knock five times."

"I hate to leave you, George," Nancy said. "How are you feeling? Are you sure you'll be all right? We could just go home and do this another night. Maybe we should take you to get that ankle looked at or x-rayed."

"Hey," George said. "I've been in sports all my life. I know a sprained ankle. There's some cloth in the cabin. I can wrap it. That'll keep the swelling down. You two go ahead—I'll be okay."

They retraced their steps to the blacksmith's cabin. George let herself in, and Nancy and Bess went on.

For the third time Nancy and Bess went through the orchard, over the old footbridge, and up the hill through the woods. This time the moon was full and very bright. Nancy also had her flashlight, so they moved quickly.

As they walked up the hill, Bess spotted another scrap of what looked like the Lantern Lady's cloak clinging to a branch. She handed it to Nancy.

"I wish I could think of what that reminds me of," Nancy muttered as she dropped it into her pocket.

When they reached the top of the hill, they stopped to look down the other side. "I can see the map in my mind," Nancy said. "I think the house and icehouse were this way."

"Sounds good to me," Bess said. "I've gotten sort of turned around."

As they neared the area, Nancy fanned her flashlight beam around. "There!" Bess said. "What's that?"

They saw a tangled pile of vines and leaves. Remembering warnings about snakes and coyotes, Nancy got a large branch and poked at the vines from a distance. She was not too surprised to discover that the vines were not growing naturally at all. They had been piled up to camouflage an old wooden door.

Cautiously, Nancy opened the creaking door. She flashed her light around to reveal a cavelike room carved into the side of the hill. There were a few old crocks and vats around to show that this had probably been the icehouse on the map.

But even more interesting—and more revealing—were the things that had obviously been added more recently.

"Look at this," Bess said breathlessly. "Lantern Lady costumes." An old chair stood against the wall. On it were piled four matching hand-made greenish white cloaks with sleeves. On the floor were a pile of candle stubs and several tin lanterns.

"That's it!" Nancy said, rushing to where Bess stood. "Of course. Why didn't I realize it sooner!"

"What? What are you talking about?"

"This fabric," Nancy said, feeling the material. "I knew it looked familiar. It's the same fabric as the solid color patches in Mabel Tansy's skirt. The one she wears as the doctor's wife."

"Mabel Tansy? Are you saying that Mabel Tansy's the Lantern Lady?"

"They wear the same fabric." Nancy cast the beam around the rest of the cavelike room. "What's this?" She reached down and picked up a crumpled piece of paper.

Bess held the flashlight as Nancy smoothed out the paper. "It's the missing drawing from the museum gallery," Nancy said. "Remember when we were cleaning up after the gallery had been vandalized? You found that sampler of a family tree, but it was so old we couldn't read it."

"And someone said that one of the museum restorers had made a drawing of it," Bess remembered. "But we never found it."

"Someone did and brought it here," Nancy said. "It's the Parrish family tree. Look at this branch. What name do you see?"

"Tansy!" Bess said with a gasp.

"Let's go," Nancy said. "I'm worried about George." She put the drawing into her pocket and started for the door. Then she turned back. "I have an idea," she said. "Put one of those cloaks in my backpack."

Bess took some of the things out of Nancy's pack and put them in hers to make room. Then she took one of the Lantern Lady cloaks from the stack of four and stuffed it into Nancy's pack.

Nancy pushed some leaves between two of the costumes in the remaining stack and plumped up the material so you couldn't tell that one was missing. Then Nancy and Bess hurried back to the smithy's cabin.

As soon as they arrived, Nancy had an uneasy feeling that something wasn't right. She signaled Bess to be quiet and stay down. Slowly they circled to the back of the cabin. "Uh-oh," Bess said in a tiny voice. The cabin door was standing wide open.

They stepped inside and looked quickly through the two small rooms. No one was there. "Maybe George is upstairs," Bess whispered. "Where we hid out earlier."

Nodding, Nancy carefully crept up the steps to the loft. She stuck her head above the stairway and looked around. George wasn't there.

"Where is she?" Bess whispered. Her voice echoed the worry that Nancy felt.

"I don't know, but we'll find her," Nancy said, her voice hushed. She and Bess scurried around outside the cabin. "George!" Nancy called in a loud whisper. "George! Where are you?"

"Nmgsee!" they heard George's muffled voice call out. "Nn hwrr!"

"The smokehouse," Bess cried. "I think she's in the smokehouse."

Nancy and Bess rushed to the small building behind the cabin. It was a one-room wooden shed with no windows and one door in front. On either side of the door were two iron L-shaped braces. A long piece of wood was cradled in the braces, barring the door. Quickly Nancy lifted the wooden bar up and out of the holders and pulled open the door.

"George!" Nancy called as Bess raced to her cousin. George was roped to a chair in the middle of the small room, with a rag tied around her mouth. As Nancy and Bess worked at unknotting the gag and ropes, the door slammed shut behind them. With a sinking heart, Nancy heard the bar drop into the holders.

14

The Trap Is Set

"Nancy!" Bess cried. "We're trapped!"

"Don't worry," Nancy said. "We'll get out of here somehow."

Bess untied the last binding holding George to the chair. Nancy loosened the knot that held the rag around George's mouth.

"I don't know who it was," George said. "Someone knocked me out while I was wrapping my ankle. When I came to, I was here."

"It was Mabel Tansy, George," Bess said. "She's the Lantern Lady. You won't believe what we found." While Nancy looked around, Bess told George about the icehouse and what was inside.

A thin shaft of moonlight plunged from the

square, screened opening at the top of the shed. Nancy remembered from her training that it was a vent, but it was too small to wriggle through.

At the bottom of the shed was a narrow opening, also screened. It was about a foot wide and six inches high. A fire would be built in a metal container outside the shed. Periodically, someone would stoke the fire to keep it hot and smoking. The smoke would flow in through that small opening and penetrate the meat hanging in the smokehouse. This would preserve the meat.

"Mabel," George said. "Wow!"

"We think so," Nancy said. "If she's part of the Parrish family, there's probably some trouble that goes way back. Something between her side and Jake Parrish's side of the family."

"Well, let's get out of here, so we can tell *everybody* about it," Bess said. She went over to the door and pushed hard. It didn't budge. Nancy could see a picture of the outside of the door in her mind. The two L-shaped braces held the bar that lay across the door, keeping it shut.

"This room is so smelly," Bess said as she went back and helped George up. About a foot above their heads, sausages, hams, turkeys, and large hunks of other meats hung from the ceiling on huge black iron hooks. The floor was slippery with fat and grease, which dripped from the drying meat.

"Is it just because I was hit on the head, or is it getting warmer in here?" George asked, rubbing the back of her neck.

Nancy looked down at the floor. A thin curl of blue-gray smoke wafted in. Then it grew thicker and darker. She went to the opening and heard someone stir the coals outside before running away.

"The fire's been started up," Nancy said. "Whoever it was has left, but we've got to keep that smoke out of here." She pulled the chair over. It slid easily on the slippery floor.

"Be careful, Nancy," Bess warned. "I'll hold the chair steady so it won't slide."

Nancy stepped on the chair and reached up. She unhooked a long slab of meat and dropped it to the floor. George kicked it over in front of the smoke opening.

Nancy studied the ceiling, then looked at the door. "You've got an idea," George said. "I can tell. Great!"

"It might work," Nancy said. "It's worth a shot." She reached for two of the huge hooks and pulled them off the nails holding them to the ceiling.

Back on the floor, she handed one to Bess. "Come on," she said. They walked to the door.

"I can help," George said.

129

"You have a sprained ankle and a conked head," Bess said. "Just stay where you are."

"Okay," Nancy said. "The bar that is lying across the door is about waist high." She pinpointed a spot on a level with her knees and said, "Let's see if we can slip these hooks between the door and the walls right about here."

Bess took one side of the door, Nancy the other. They pushed and jiggled the huge iron hooks through the narrow cracks where the sides of the door met the walls of the old shed. "Now pull the hook up. We want to lift the bar and roll it out of its holders."

Nancy and Bess pulled the hooks up along the sides of the door. They could feel the bar when they got to it. And they could tell they were lifting it by how much harder their work was. Finally they felt the bar roll up and out of the holders, and they heard it rattle onto the ground.

Nancy pushed the door open. The three rushed out, taking huge gulps of clean air. "We'll never get that smell out of our noses or clothes or hair," Bess said, her nose scrunched up.

"Sure we will," George said. "A long shower will do wonders."

"About an hour long," Nancy said, looking around. "Be careful. I know we heard someone running away from here earlier, but that doesn't mean we're alone now."

Bess and Nancy walked slowly around the smokehouse, while George leaned against the wall, keeping her weight off her twisted ankle.

"Keep an eye out while I check the smokehouse fire," Nancy said. She made sure the fire was out, then brought George the door bar. "You'd better use this as a walking stick," Nancy told her friend. "Your ankle is really swollen."

Cautiously, the three fanned out. Using trees and shrubs as shields, they made their way through the blacksmith's backyard and around to the front of the cabin.

"Well, there's no sign of the guard or Mabel," Nancy whispered at last. "Let's get out of here." Quickly they headed for the car.

On the way home all three sighed with relief. "We're sweaty, smoky, and smelly," Bess said.

"But safe," George added.

Friday morning Nancy picked up Bess and George in her Mustang. The smell of smoked meat still filled her car and reminded her of the previous night's dangers. As George limped out to the car, Nancy was happy to see that his bandaged ankle was definitely better.

On the drive to the village, they talked about the next step in their investigation.

"I'm sure Mabel is the Lantern Lady," Nancy said, "but she probably doesn't know we suspect her. Let's all be really friendly and win her confidence. Make sure she doesn't realize we know what's going on. Then we can set our own trap."

"Does it have something to do with the costume you took from the icehouse?" George asked.

"Mm-hmm," Nancy answered, nodding. "The hayrides are tonight, right?"

"That's right," Bess said. "It's Friday. The tourists are going to get hayrides through the orchard and along the river like the one we took the first night we were here."

"Do you think Mabel will make an appearance as the Lantern Lady again?" George asked.

"I sure do," Nancy answered. Remember how frightened the horse was? And how people were tossed out into the ditch? It's a perfect way to cause trouble and get more publicity."

"So?" Bess said. "What's your plan?"

"How do you suppose Mabel will feel if she sees her *own* ghost?" Nancy asked, smiling.

"Two Lantern Ladies?" George said. "I love it."

"Let's wait until we find out where Bess and I will be assigned today," Nancy said. "Then we'll work out the plan."

When they got to the village, Nancy was happy to learn she was going back to the doctor's house.

She knew that would help her win Mabel's confidence. Plus she could keep track of the woman. George would be at the smithy's cabin, of course. Bess and Cory were assigned to help Amy at the general store.

When Nancy arrived, Mabel was laying out the doctor's instruments. She looked at Nancy carefully. She seemed to be studying her, as if she was trying to read Nancy's mind.

"Oh, Mabel," Nancy said, talking fast. "You won't believe what happened to a few of us last night. It was horrible!"

"Really?" Mabel said, folding her hands in front of her. She seemed to be nervous, and she watched Nancy closely.

"Well," Nancy began, "now don't be mad—and please don't tell Mr. Parrish. A few of us thought it would be fun to stay after hours. Just to see what it was like. We figured it would be safe, especially with the traders and their families camped in the meadow."

Nancy took a deep breath. "Anyway, we hid out until everyone left. Then we were just looking around and we got trapped in the smoke-house!"

Mabel's cheeks flushed a faint pink and her body seemed to stiffen a little. It was as if she was suddenly on guard. "What do you mean, you were trapped?" she asked.

"We were locked in," Nancy said. "And we're sure it was the Lantern Lady. You know, I never believed in ghosts before, but I do now. We were so scared. Boy, that's the last time I ever do anything that stupid."

"The Lantern Lady, hmm? You say you're sure that's what it was?"

"It had to have been. Who else could it be? If it had been the guard or one of the other employees, they would have kicked us out—and probably fired us." Nancy glanced down and shook her head. When she looked up again, she saw that Mabel had relaxed a little.

"No, it had to be the Lantern Lady," Nancy said. "I hate to say this, but I'm glad I signed on for only this week. I don't think I could be a regular here, with that ghost wandering around all the time. How do you do it? Aren't you scared?"

"Well, no," Mabel said. Her posture softened, and she even smiled a little. "The Lantern Lady has never . . . I mean . . . well . . . I . . ." She stopped for a minute, then shook her finger at Nancy. "Maybe that will teach you a lesson, young lady," she said. "You and your friends should never have been around here after hours. Who was with you?"

"If possible, I'd rather not tell you," Nancy said. "I'm willing to take full responsibility. It

134

was my idea. Believe me, it won't happen again."
Nancy picked up the broom. "Why don't I sweep
the floors before the tourists arrive?"

She left the doctor's office before Mabel could
speak and began straightening up the parlor.
Nancy took another deep breath as she worked
her way into the dining room. So far, so good, she
thought. She was sure Mabel didn't suspect that
Nancy knew the truth about the Lantern Lady.

The rest of the day went smoothly, and by late
afternoon the village was filled with tourists
lining up for the hayrides. There would be six
hay wagons, and the rides would begin as soon as
the sun started to set. A half hour before they
were to start, Mabel told Nancy that she had to
help with the wagon loading. She asked Nancy to
take over as hostess at the doctor's house.

The plan called for George to keep an eye on
the doctor's house from the smithy's cabin across
the street. If she saw Mabel leave, she was to go
over to the doctor's house.

Nancy finished talking to a few tourists and
ushered them out the back door as George came
into the kitchen. She was using old wooden
crutches that Amy had found in the back of the
general store. "You look very authentic," Nancy
said, smiling.

"I feel authentic," George said with a mock
frown. "A little too authentic, actually." She

sank down onto the parlor settee. "It only hurts when I move."

"Then stay off that foot," Nancy advised. "Just greet the tourists as they come through. I know you can handle it."

"No problem," George said, propping her foot up on a red-flowered footstool. "There probably won't be that many tourists walking around now anyway. Most of them will be lining up for the hayrides. I'll just tell them that the doctor's wife is helping him on a call, and I've come over to 'mind things,' as Mabel would say."

"Speaking of Mabel, I've got to go," Nancy said. "Wish us luck." She left the doctor's house and went to the Visitors Center. She grabbed the Lantern Lady costume she had taken from the icehouse and put it into a large burlap bag. Then she carried the bag back up the village path to the general store.

When she got to the general store, Nancy told Amy that she and Bess had to run an errand. She borrowed two lanterns and some matches, and she and Bess left for the orchard.

"Nancy, you're sure it's Mabel and not a ghost?" Bess asked with a shudder as they walked.

"Yes," Nancy said. "I really am."

"Okay then," Bess said, her eyes flashing in the waning twilight. "Let's catch her."

Nancy and Bess walked past the meadow to the thick orchard near the old footbridge across the river. While Bess watched the river from behind the trees, Nancy put on the Lantern Lady costume. The large cloak completely covered her dress. She removed her bonnet and pulled the hood of the cloak up over her head. It draped down over the top of her face just as the Lantern Lady's did. She was sure that, in the dark, no one would recognize her.

"Cool," Bess said when Nancy came out from behind a tree. "You look like the real thing."

"How about when I move?" Nancy asked, taking a few steps and turning.

"It's perfect," Bess murmured. "That cloak completely hides your shoes. When you move, you really look as if you're floating."

In the distance, they could hear the horses and see the hay wagons filling with tourists.

"Nancy," Bess called in a loud whisper. "Look! Across the river on the hill."

Nancy looked in the direction Bess pointed. She could see a bobbing light moving slowly down the hill. Then she turned to look back toward the village. The first hay wagon of tourists rumbled into the orchard.

Using the trees for cover, Nancy and Bess crept through the orchard to the old footbridge. Then they ducked into the underbrush at the edge of the bridge. They waited, watching the moving light across the river until it reached the bottom of the hill.

"There she is," Bess whispered.

Nancy reached down and lit one of the lanterns, keeping it concealed under the bridge. Her pulse pounded in her head under the draped hood.

Across the river the Lantern Lady stepped on to the far end of the footbridge. She stood very still. For a moment it was if the world had stopped and there was nothing but an eerie hush. Nancy watched, her breath coming in short gasps. She knew she had to wait until just the right moment to make her move.

Then the ghostly figure began swinging her lantern slowly from side to side as she moved forward across the bridge. As the Lantern Lady approached, the only sound Nancy heard was her own racing heartbeat.

15

The Legend Ends?

The Lantern Lady moved slowly forward over the bridge. Screams and yells from the orchard pierced the silence, and Nancy felt a bolt of energy shoot through her. "Here I go," she mumbled to Bess.

Carefully Nancy took the lantern and stepped up out of the underbrush and onto the footbridge. It was if she were looking into a mirror. Slowly, she swung her lantern from side to side as she moved forward.

More shouts filled the air. For a moment Nancy lost her concentration. She pictured what the scene must look like—two ghostly Lantern Ladies moving toward each other.

Suddenly the real Lantern Lady stopped. She dropped her light and brought her hands to her mouth. The tin lantern clattered across the bridge and disappeared through a hole. With a sizzling plop it fell into the river.

The Lantern Lady took a few steps backward, then turned and ran off the bridge. Nancy pulled off her own heavy cloak and dropped it in a heap. Then she grabbed her lantern and carefully ran across the bridge. She could hear Bess behind her.

When they reached the other side of the bridge, the Lantern Lady was halfway up the hill.

"We know where she's going. Right, Nancy?"

"We sure do," Nancy said. "Come on."

By the time they reached the top of the hill, there was no sign of the Lantern Lady. By the light from the lanterns, they made their way down to the pile of dead vines that covered the icehouse door.

"I'm sure she's in there," Nancy murmured. She was cautious as she slowly pushed open the old wooden door. "Mabel?" she called out. "Are you here? It's Nancy Drew."

She opened the door wider and held up her light. The Lantern Lady was sitting on the chair on top of the extra costumes. Her hood was hanging over her shoulders, revealing the face of

Mabel Tansy. Her eyes were wide with shock as she stared at the lantern.

"It's over, Mabel," Nancy said gently, taking Mabel's arm. "Let's go back to the village."

Mabel rambled on about seeing a ghost, about seeing the real Lantern Lady across the bridge. Bess tried to tell her it was Nancy, but she didn't seem to understand.

Nancy turned Mabel over to the guard at the Visitors Center. She asked him to hold Mabel, briefly filling him in and explaining that she was going to get Jake Parrish. Mabel was still mumbling to herself and didn't seem to hear or understand what Nancy was saying.

Nancy found Jake at the wagon loading spot. It took several minutes to pull him away from the crowd and explain what had happened. By the time she and Jake got to the Visitors Center, the guard had called the police. Bess had gotten George, and they were all waiting for Nancy.

Nancy explained how she and her friends had figured out Mabel's icehouse hiding place, then set the trap to catch her.

When Mabel saw Jake, she leaped out of her chair toward him. "You!" she screamed. "It's all your fault. You and your side of the family."

Jake took a step backward, his face white. "What are you talking about? What's the matter with you?"

141

"I'm your cousin, you fool," she said. "You Parrishes duped the Tansys out of their rightful inheritance. That old icehouse was ours. That whole hill and half this village property was ours. But your grandfather pulled a fast one and we were left with nothing. Nothing!" Her mouth curled down in an ugly snarl.

"So you decided to get back at my grandfather by ruining Persimmon Woods?" Jake said. "That doesn't make any sense."

"As a duty to my family I'm bound to close this place down," Mabel said. "You're not going to make money off the Tansys any longer." She turned to Nancy, saying, "My plan would have worked, too, if you hadn't volunteered for the festival."

"Did you leave the message on my phone machine?" Nancy asked Mabel.

"And did you knock me out and lock us in the smokehouse last night?" George added.

Mabel nodded curtly. "You were snooping around," Mabel said. "I was sure of it. I thought I'd scare you off. I didn't intend to hurt you."

"You've done it all by yourself?" Jake asked. "Dumped the coverlets and pottery in the river? Made the bomb threat? Torn apart the gallery and the gift shop? Even the musket accident?"

"Yes!" Mabel said. "I had to. I didn't mean for anyone to get hurt."

142

The police arrived and took Mabel away. "I don't know how to thank you," Jake said to Nancy. "But I'm sure we'll think of something." Then he sighed. "Well, I have to get back to the hayrides. You three are welcome to go back to the village or go on home if you'd rather. The park is closing soon anyway."

Nancy, Bess, and George decided to go back to their posts and work for the last hour. But they agreed not to say anything to anyone about what had happened. "We should let Jake Parrish handle the announcement," Nancy pointed out.

Nancy found it very strange to be in the doctor's house without Mabel. She even felt a little sad.

The locker room was buzzing with rumors when Nancy went to change. Some of the villagers had seen the police take Mabel away. "What's it all about?" Amy asked Nancy breathlessly as they put their bonnets up on the rack. "Was Mabel really the Lantern Lady? Everyone says so."

"We can't really talk about it right now, Amy," Nancy said. "Maybe tomorrow. Let's wait and see what happens next, okay?"

"Okay," Amy said as they walked out to the parking lot. Bess and George followed but more slowly. George had left her crutches in the locker room and was leaning on Bess's shoulder for support.

"But Cory is sure you were the second Lantern Lady," Amy persisted. "At least tell us that. It was you, wasn't it?"

"Yes," Bess blurted out. "That much we can admit. Didn't Nancy make a great Lantern Lady?"

"I knew it," Cory said, joining them. "I knew it was Nancy. It was a trap, wasn't it? To capture the real Lantern Lady?"

"At least tell us—was it Mabel who has been causing all the trouble around here?" Amy asked. "Why did the police take her away?"

"We really can't say any more right now," Nancy said as she unlocked her car. "Maybe tomorrow. We'll see you then."

Saturday morning was sunny. George and Bess arrived at Nancy's house early for breakfast. While they dug into a stack of Hannah's pancakes, they passed around the newspaper. The headline story told about the unmasking of the Lantern Lady at Persimmon Woods Pioneer Village.

"I'm going to give Anita a call after breakfast," Carson said. "She can take that moving truck back to the rental place. I've arranged a loan for her so she won't lose her home."

As if on cue, there was a knock on the door. Nancy walked Anita into the kitchen and set a place for her at the table.

"I was just talking about you," Nancy's father said. He repeated his good news. "I've also talked to a few friends and associates. A couple of them would like to talk to you about a job."

Nancy could see the tears well up in Anita's eyes. "Thank you so much, Carson. It's been really hard lately. When my father died, he left a lot of debts. I've been trying to pay them off, and it's been a real struggle. But I didn't embezzle any money!"

Anita smiled warmly at Nancy's father. "It was a lucky day when I moved near you and Nancy," she said. "And you, too, Hannah. These are the best pancakes I've ever tasted."

Anita gulped some coffee. "I have news, too," she said. "That's why I'm here. Guess who called me this morning."

"Well, it couldn't have been the Lantern Lady," George said. "She's been put out of business."

"It was Jake Parrish," Anita said. "He promised to set the record straight."

"So he knows you didn't embezzle any money?" Nancy said.

"Yeah," Anita said. "Because *he* was the one fiddling with the numbers. He just got rid of me so I wouldn't find out. Then, in case anyone else did, he planted the idea that I was the culprit."

"That's terrible," Bess said. "What a mean thing to do."

"And illegal," Carson added.

"Actually, nothing's been embezzled. He says he didn't really steal any money. He's just been moving it around from one account to another. Since Mabel started pulling her tricks out there, attendance has gone way down. He tried to hide the fact that the revenue had dropped so much."

"So what's he going to do about it?" George asked.

"He's says he'll throw himself on the mercy of the board of directors—tell them everything and hope they give him another chance. He seems sure they will. After all, Mabel's out of the picture now. With the danger gone, attendance ought to climb again. And guess what else."

"He offered you your old job back," Nancy said, adding more syrup to her last pancake.

"You are a good detective," Anita replied with a laugh. "You're right. He offered to talk to the board about taking me back."

"What did you say?" Bess asked. "I sure wouldn't go back after all he put you through."

"I feel the same way, Bess," Anita said. "I told him I'd think about it, but I don't really want to go back. Now, thanks to you, Carson, I might not have to."

Beep-beep-ba-beep-beep. A vehicle horn sounded in the driveway. "That must be Cory and Amy," Bess said, jumping up. "They called me earlier and offered to pick us all up here."

"I'll never forget the sight of Nancy and Mabel moving toward each other on the bridge," Amy said as Cory drove them to Persimmon Woods.

"Wasn't it eerie?" Bess said, her voice low.

"Yeah," Cory said. "It was like two knights with swords getting ready to duke it out in a joust. Only it was ghosts with lanterns."

"I'm sorry for Mabel," Bess said. "I hope she gets some help. She seems pretty mixed up."

"I'm sorry for her, too," Cory said. "But it's been pretty scary around here for a while and getting worse. Especially with bomb scares. She was determined to ruin the village, and she had to be stopped."

"I agree," Amy said. "Persimmon Woods is very important to this area. It would have been a terrible loss if she had succeeded in destroying it."

When they arrived, they found that Jake Parrish had gathered the villagers in the reception area of the Visitors Center. Cheers and applause greeted them as Nancy, Bess, George, and the Worths walked in.

When all the villagers had arrived, Jake said he had a few announcements. "First of all," he began, "I'm sure you all know about Mabel. She was a dedicated worker here for many years. Many of you probably consider her a friend. She says she never meant to hurt anyone, and we believe her. We are going to do everything we can to help her.

"Nancy," he continued, "you've been here less than a week, but we consider you, Bess, and George valued members of the Persimmon Woods family. All of us thank you for ending the destruction that was tearing away at our village."

He shook Nancy's hand. "It's hard to express enough thanks for what you've done for Persimmon Woods," he continued. "You, George, and Bess will always have a home here. Any time you want to step back in time and be a part of us, you are welcome. You each will have lifetime passes, in case you just want to visit."

"Thank you," Nancy said, smiling. "We were really happy to be able to help."

"George, your ankle is mending, I hope," Jake said. "We especially appreciate your sacrifice for our cause."

"It's much better, thanks," George said. "And I think it was worth it."

"Believe me, it will be," Jake said. "The board of directors for Persimmon Woods was about to announce a reward for information leading to the identity of the person causing all the problems around here. So you three will be receiving more than just our verbal thanks."

Jake turned to the group, saying, "Well, you'd better get in your costumes. The tourists will be here soon. I think we can expect a larger than usual number today. You know, I have just one regret. This place won't be quite the same without the Lantern Lady."

"Maybe you should hire someone to play her part," Cory suggested. "How about Nancy? She gave quite an audition out on that bridge."

"She'd be perfect," Bess chimed in. "After all, she was assigned to be a *floater!*"